Zao, Olymbris, Thoorana, Zephrondus, and Great Gulzund;
These five worlds circle the star Kylix in the Unicorn.

Now it is of Zao that I would speak.

No eye but mine hath seen her walled stone cities, her green magicians, her fabulous beasts.

But I have voyaged thither in my dreams, and from that far voyaging I bring back to you this tale. . . .

—Song of Worlds, from
THE CHRONICLES OF KYLIX,
the Second Book.

THE WIZARD OF ZAO

Lin Carter

DAW BOOKS, INC.
DONALD A. WOLLHEIM, PUBLISHER

1301 Avenue of the Americas
New York, N. Y. 10019

Cover art by Carl Lundgren.

For Amy . . .

"All people are alone in some ways; some people are alone in all ways."

—*Now, Voyager*

FIRST PRINTING, JUNE 1978

1 2 3 4 5 6 7 8 9

PRINTED IN U.S.A.

The Contents

I. The Wizard and the Wild Girl

II. The Simurgh and the Shebites

III. Gamar and the Goblins

Glash, a Village called Yan, and a Captive Warrior known as Gomar. *8:* Discusses the History of the Sword Adamanta, Describes the Journey South into Yab, and Contains Some Very Interesting Philosophical Meditations. *9:* How Our Friends were Taken Captive by Gluth the Unspeakable, of the Goblin King and His Repulsive Court, and How the Wizard Volunteered to Assist in the Conquest of Yab.

IV. Vroop and Victory

10: In Which we Enjoy the Rare Opportunity of Observing a Duel between Magicians, of the Outcome Thereof, and in Which Gamar Begins to Develop Suspicions. *11:* Concerns Several Various Escapes and Captures, and in Which the Wizard Plots the Destruction of Shang, and Enters the City Presumably for That Purpose. *12:* In Which Wars—and Thrones—are Lost and Won, Hidden Identities are At Last Revealed, and Gamar, or Amar, Guesses the Wizard's Own Secret but Says Nothing.

*

The Afterword: In Which, After the Usual Coronations and Weddings and Banquets and Victory Speeches, and All That Sort of Thing, Our Friends Part—Each to His or Her Own Particular Destiny, and the Wizard Goes Home to Mount Wu. To Which the Author Has Thoughtfully Appended a Note.

I.

THE WIZARD AND THE WILD GIRL

1.

In which a Number of Pazools Change Hands, a Wizard Gets a Chela, and a Slave Girl is Purchased by a Most Unusual Master

They usually close the gates of Ning at sunset and thereafter permit no travelers to enter the Purple City. But they made an exception in the Wizard's case.

The reason for this policy is simple economy, nothing else. Although the Purple City of Ning rises on the edges of a desert called The Desolation of Yu, the Ningivites have nothing to fear from desert raiders. And although the Emperor of Ning has somehow or other managed to make enemies of each of his neighboring monarchs, the Ningivites have nothing to fear from war or invasion.

This is because there is no money in Ning.

And only idiots make war against a city that is as poor as Ning is poor. Hence they consider themselves invulnerable. And the Emperor, whose name is Thang, frequently refers to himself as "Thang the Unconquerable," although his brother sovereigns for several kingdoms around call him "Thang the Pauper."

So this is why the gates were closed and locked at sunset. Gates have to be guarded, if only so the Emperor has somebody there to collect an entrance fee from every visitor. And guards have to be paid. Especially, guards who are asked to work both day *and* night. The Emperor had the choice of either paying his gate guards time-and-a-half overtime, or hiring special guards to work the night shift. It seemed simpler just to lock the gates and keep the money.

"A *pazool* saved is a *pazool* earned," was the Emperor's motto.

He was very fond of *pazools*, the Emperor.

The guards had already locked the seven locks and were closing up the guardhouse when the Wizard came riding up on a fat, waddling scarlet lizard.

The Wizard was fat, too, and, had he been afoot, he would probably have waddled also. He was quite an odd-looking fellow, which is how wizards ought to look, come to think of it. This particular Wizard was apple green, quite fat, and bald as an egg, except for a braided queue of ink-black hair which grew from a topknot in the very center of his pate, and hung down his back.

He had wobbling jowls, clean-shaven, a jolly smile, sleepy—but clever—slitted black eyes under ironic, pencil-thin, arched brows, and several chins, the uppermost of which was adorned by a very small, very neat black pointed beard the size and shape of an arrowhead.

This was all of him the guards could see, the rest being wrapped in a dusty red robe, red being the color of magic on this planet, whose name, by the way, was Zao. It happens to be the second planet of the star Kylix in the Constellation of the Unicorn, and a most unique world it is, as you will soon discover.

Well, the Wizard asked to be let in but the guards told him to come back in the morning, as the gates were closed till then.

"What time are you supposed to close the gates, boys?" he inquired affably.

"Sunset."

"Ah! Good. Then I can still get in," said the Wizard.

That puzzled them a bit. They leaned over the crenellations, resting their elbows lazily on the worn purple stone, and asked him how he figured that.

Reaching behind him into a knapsack and drawing forth a fat black jug which he uncorked and from which he took a swig of liquid refreshment, he took his time before answering.

"Well, 'sunset' is very imprecise," he said expansively. "What does it mean, after all? 'When the sun goes down,' you might say. Yes, but how do you know when the sun goes down? Now, it may go down here in Ning at seven o'clock . . . but a thousand miles due west of here, in the city of Xang, it is still, at this moment, an hour *before* sunset. So, you see, my friends, 'sunset' is a *relative* term, and hence cannot be perfectly defined . . . what you Ningivites call sunset, my dear friends the Xangians call late afternoon. Since I myself have the honor to be a native-born Xangian, you really ought to let me in!"

One of the guards listening to this turned to his captain and remarked that they had better let him in, if only to stop him from talking, as the Wizard seemed liable to go on all night, and he (the guard, that is), for one, wanted to get home in time for supper.

So they made an exception to the rule and opened the gates for the green-skinned Wizard, who thumped his heels into the plump, scaly ribs of his lazy lizard until, puffing out its throat in outrage, it waddled through the gates and into the city.

By way of thanks, the Wizard, after paying the entrance toll, which was two *pazools*, performed a minor feat of magic. After several mysterious gestures and a sentence in a particularly unknown tongue, the Wizard reached up and drew a third gold *pazool* from the guard captain's left ear, which he graciously permitted the officer to keep, asking only that he buy a drink for the boys with it.

Then, having solicited directions to the slave bazaar, he affably bid the guards goodnight and kicked his sleepy lizard awake, ambling off down a crooked little street.

Although a small and rather miserable little city badly in need of repainting, Ning was not without quaintness, and as his scarlet lizard puffed along, the Wizard took in what sights there were with a comfortable smile and an interested eye.

Ning had crooked, narrow, cobblestone streets and little five-sided houses with pointed windows and peaked roofs, and every few blocks you came upon a small square with a splashing fountain where slave girls were filling the water jugs, and these girls giggled to see the fat, grinning, bald green wizard on the puffing scarlet lizard, and the Wizard gave them a special grin and even a wink or two, especially the pretty ones.

He had spent the last month with the desert raiders. They are a grim, silent, dour, puritanical people and live in black felt tents and dress in scratchy black robes and all of their women, even the young and pretty ones, wear hoods in which eye-holes have been cut so that they can see out but you can't see in. That is, the most you can see is a pair of eyes. So the Wizard was happy to see a pretty face or two and a slim tanned ankle.

He halted his lizard at the slave bazaar, which was still open for business even though it was rapidly getting dark, and watched the proceedings for a while with lazy interest.

They had hung paper lanterns out so that the customers could get a good look at the merchandise, and since the merchandise consisted almost entirely of pretty young girls, and since the pretty young girls went almost entirely without clothes, you can understand how important good lighting was to the progress of the sales.

Business was going quite well as the Wizard pulled his fat scaly steed to a halt in the rear of the crowd and, from his high padded saddle, looked over the heads of the customers at the slave block. A fat, purple-skinned slave master, who wore an embroidered vest, a gold ring in his left ear, and voluminous pantaloons striped peach and rose, had just disposed of a matched pair of thirteen-year-old twins for a nice price, and loudly called for the attention of his audience and commanded his assistant to bring out the next item.

A murmur of surprise arose from the audience as the next item emerged from the tent behind the block. For it was a Wild Girl; quite a pretty girl, but Wild as wild could be. Her shining black hair was a tousled mass of ringlets. Her blazing dark eyes were furious and they glared back and forth across the audience, raking it with scornful contempt. Her luscious, ripe mouth was pursed in a rebellious expression. The rest of her was rather ripe and luscious, too, and since her entire costume consisted of a string of red beads, it was easy to see that she was a genuine collector's item. In fact, the slave master, Zool the Soft-Hearted by name, pointed this out.

"My next item, O Masters of Generously Filled Purses, is a true collector's item for the discriminating connoisseur! Yes sir, a genuine Wild Girl from the Barbarian Mountains beyond the trackless plains of Chun! Captured at no small expense, I assure you, by none other than that intrepid master slaver, Thog the Fearless, at great risk to life and limb! The tale of Master Thog's daring expedition deep into Barbarian country is material for an epic, that it is, but—come! I know you are not here to listen to an epic, but for reasons of business, eh? Business, or perhaps—" (a smirk and a broad wink) "—possibly, *pleasure?* If so, O Possessors of Lusty Loins, you have come to the right slave emporium, for never in many years has so choice a juicy morsel of girlflesh passed through my hands—to yours—as this delicious, untamed, fiery-spirited wench! Just notice, if you will, how those red beads are set off by the smooth, satiny, tawny, dusky flesh wherewith they are surrounded! And notice, as well, the round, firm, temptingly elastic, proud, jiggling . . ."

As Zool the Soft-Hearted warmed to his task of describing that which needed no description (since it was standing right there in full view of everybody, arms akimbo, dark eyes flashing through rebellious locks, under the paper lanterns), his eloquence waxed enthusiastic, then rhapsodic. The green Wizard, fond of good rhetoric, listened with judicious approval, beaming appreciatively. And when the slave master concluded his presentation, the Wizard bid ten gold *pazools*—a generous sum, in fact, a princely bid. So princely, that the bachelor Ningivites clustered about—being as poor as most Ningivites—could not top his bid, and bent sour looks upon him as he dismounted, wheezing, and waddled through the throng to pay the price and to collect his purchase.

The Wizard did not really have ten gold *pazools* in his pouch, but the slave master did not know this.

"Ah!" exclaimed Zool, as the Wizard emerged from the crowd into his view, "if I am not woefully incorrect, I believe the generous bidder of ten *pazools* is none other than a gentleman-practitioner of the Art Sorcerous! Perhaps your Wizardry would favor your fellow customers with a small feat of admirable legerdemain, before vanishing into the night with this adorable armful of Barbarian girlhood?"

I should perhaps explain here that most Wizards of this planet, Zao, have apple-green skin. The green race of Zao dwell in the Seven Magical Kingdoms which center around Mount Wu, otherwise known as "Magic Mountain." Since sorcery is in the very air they breathe, and infused into the very soil of the Seven Kingdoms, most of the green race turn naturally to the practice of that art. Hence the Zaoites of other races automatically assume that any Green Zaoite they meet is one or another kind of a magician. And they are usually right.

"Well, now, I don't mind if I do," the Wizard grinned. He frowned thoughtfully, pursed his lips, rubbed his brow, fingered his tiny neat beardlet, tugged on his queue, and said: "If you good people would kindly reach down and pick up some pebbles from the ground and hand them to me, I'll see if I can't . . . thank you, sir . . . thank you . . . thank you *so* much . . . no, I think these ten pebbles will do nicely . . . now then! If you will all kindly pay attention . . . you will see I have nothing up my sleeve . . . now: I close my fingers over this handful of pebbles and blow on them like this, *whoosh,* and recite the magic phrase, *Abracadabra! Allacazam! Presto Change-oh!* And here you are, slave master, the correct purchase price, unless I am very much mistaken?"

Five fat green fingers curled open to show ten glittering coins, stamped with the profile portrait, somewhat idealized, of Thang IV, Emperor of All Ning.

Zool crowed ecstatically, and enthusiastically led the small, polite patter of applause. Of course, he thought the Wizard had worked a small trick of sleight-of-hand, palming the pebbles somehow. He collected the coins, bit one or two of them, thanked the Wizard effusively, handed over the Wild Girl, bid the Wizard good-night, and was very much surprised, later on that evening, when totaling up the proceeds of the day's business, to discover ten common pebbles among his monies.

The Wizard's magic was real magic. But it only lasted when he put his mind to it.

The Wizard ambled through the crowd, leading his new slave by a leash looped around her wrists (which were tied behind her back so she couldn't scratch out the eyes of her purchaser), until he was well away from the slave bazaar. He drew from his knapsack a voluminous red robe, identical to the one he wore himself (it was his good robe, in fact, the clean one without any patches, the one he saved for Royal Command Performances), tossed it over her head, got it on her body with some difficulty, mounted his lizard again, and rode off out of the bazaar, the girl trotting along behind him.

Just beyond a small, run-down temple dedicated to The God in His aspect of Shagoor the Nimble-Fingered, Patron of Thieves, Robbers, Bandits and All Lawyers, he drew before a ramshackle inn called, rather temptingly, The Full Belly, guided his sleepy lizard into the courtyard, went in and hired a room for the night, which came to one *pazool* (he had picked up another pebble on the way in).

A dirty-faced stable boy led the lizard off to kennels in the rear. The Wizard led his new purchase into the inn and up a flight of creaking wooden stairs into his room. The room was small, cramped, airless, dirty, and hot, being located immediately under the eaves. There were no beds, and no furniture at all, except for a rickety wooden table with three and a half legs. The greasy stump of an expired candle stood in a puddle of brown wax on a cracked saucer. Such sleeping arrangements as there were consisted of one heap of sour-smelling straw, which was strewn in the corner. The sanitary facilities were in the corner opposite, and they consisted of one chipped jug, which, the Wizard did not doubt, probably served as a container for drinking water at other times. All in all, he considered himself rather overcharged, and got his revenge by ordering the cheapest possible dinner (which came with the room, and which was a loaf of stale black bread, one thin wedge of red cheese, and two miniscule wooden cups of sour beer). Dinner was slapped down on the wobble-legged table shortly thereafter by a freckled serving girl with smudged face, dirty apron, filthy hands, and a runny nose. The girl peered at the fat Wizard, and the tied-up Wild Girl, rolled her eyes as if envisioning scenes of unimaginable amatory prowess, burst into a storm of snuffling giggles and left the room under the Wizard's stern eye.

The door shut and securely latched, the Wizard relaxed, kicked off his sandals, blew his nose, scratched his tummy, all the while paying absolutely no attention to his wild-eyed captive.

The Wild Girl, whose name was Ooo, watched her new master with a rare mixture of suspicion, contempt, and curiosity. She had never been a slave before and had no idea what was about to happen to her, except, of course, Bed.

She had no particular objections to Bed, which she had experienced several times before in her short young life (she was fifteen), starting first when she was seven and had rolled in the gorse with her precocious nine-year-old brother, and a number of times after that with some of the better-looking young hunters of the tribe, with whom she had cooperated willingly, if not enthusiastically, and, unwillingly, with one scrawny and bad-smelling old reprobate of the tribe, known to the local girls as Ug Wug Gak, which means Dirty Old Man, and who had come up behind her when she wasn't looking and nearly brained her with a stone.

She had rather enjoyed Bed with the young ones. She didn't know whether she had enjoyed it with Dirty Old Man or not, having been unconscious the whole time. But she didn't think it would be much fun with the Wizard. He was too fat and probably extremely old . . . at fifteen, anything past twenty seems extremely old: but in point of fact the Wizard was so old she would have been completely astounded if she had known just *how* old he was.

At any rate, the Wizard was thinking of Food at the moment, not Bed.

He fish-eyed the unappetizing meal, and then, still paying not the least attention to his slave, worked magic upon it. Since there was no audience looking on, except for his slave, who certainly didn't count, he dispensed with the mystic gestures and mysterious words, and merely said "Chairs" and snapped his fingers in a businesslike manner.

Two chairs appeared out of thin air. The girl's eyes widened. There had been no magician in her tribe, except one old toothless geezer of a shaman who could not even conjure up rain when it was needed and who was usually sleeping off a drunk when any tribe member wanted a bit of magic done. She was quite impressed. The chairs looked marvelously comfy. They were capacious and carved of delicate ivory, and had very fat velvet cushions.

Next the Wizard said "Dinner" and snapped his fingers again. The black bread and cups of beer vanished, and were instantly replaced by a huge platter of worked gold on which a magnificent steak reposed steaming in a puddle of its own juices, two golden-brown roast fowls stuffed with mouth-watering truffles, and a slim, fluted crystal goblet filled to the brim with a superb red wine, and crusted with frost.

The Wizard made a rude noise, and snapped his fingers again.

"For two, stupid!" he said. A second dinner appeared on the other side of the table, identical to the first, even to the amount of frost on the wine goblet. The Wild Girl swallowed saliva hungrily, her eyes gleaming. It looked like being bought by *this* master was not going to be so unpleasant, after all!

Then the Wizard stretched out his hand, said "Knife," closed his fingers on a gleaming blade, and came at her.

For just an instant she tensed all over like a superb and untame young animal, and all but drew back her luscious red lips in a warning snarl: but before she realized it he had waddled around behind her and was cutting through the strap that bound her wrists together.

As she stood there—free—rubbing her slightly chafed wrists and letting the circulation come tingling back into her numb fingers, he pointed to the table (the knife, by the way, had slowly melted back into thin air again without being so commanded, obviously aware that he no longer required its services). The Wizard said, "Eat. And don't try to stab me with the steak knife and climb out of the window, because I will turn you into an amphisbaena if you try it."

An amphisbaena is a small, remarkably ugly reptile with a reputation for having bad breath. It resembles a small lizard with a head at both ends of its body. Which is to say that it lacks those rear organs wherethrough more fortunate creatures relieve themselves of body wastes (if you stop and think of it, you'd probably have bad breath, too, under the same circumstances).

Nobody in his or her right mind could possibly want to be an amphisbaena. So the Wild Girl sat docilely opposite him and ate and drank as if ravenous, which she probably was, while he talked lazily.

"I doubt if you wanted to be bought by anyone, my dear *chela,* but you are particularly fortunate that I bought you, because if I had not come along exactly when I did a scout from the palace would have come around to survey the available merchandise one minute later, would have bought you for a song and you would have ended up in the Emperor's harem. And you would most emphatically not have enjoyed life in the Emperor's harem. Thang the Unconquerable, you see, has a Thing about whippings, and he particularly likes to watch young Wild Girls being whipped—or even young Wild Boys, for that matter, being a monarch of most impartial tastes. He would have taken quite a fancy to you, my dear *chela,* and you would probably have ended up as minced meat for the palace pets in two weeks or so, and that would have been a waste, for you are very pretty: much too pretty to be used up by an old hoot who likes to watch pretty girls squirm and squeal under the lash."

The girl gave him a scornful glance and snarled, as best she could around an immense mouthful of utterly delicious steak, "Hah! *You,* I suppose, bought me from pure altruism alone!"

She accompanied this remark with an exaggerated sneer, as best she could sneer with her mouth stuffed with tender, exquisitely spiced and broiled steak. He smiled and shook his head.

"Not really. There are, or must be, hundreds of captive girls, and boys, too, being bought by cruel or capricious masters all over Zao every day. If I were an altruist, I suppose I should go around buying them all up; but such is not the case, and I would not do it even if I had the *pazools* to make it possible. No, indeed, I have a Use in mind for you."

"*I* know," she said, with an ugly grimace. "*Bed.*"

"Yes, I suppose so, if I still feel like it after this meal; but other purposes come to mind as well. Those we will have to wait and see about."

Then, abruptly changing the topic of conversation without the slightest warning, which was one of the Wizard's habits, as his new *chela* would soon learn, he began a long, rambling and rather entertaining dissertation upon the royal history of Ning, which explained why the monarch of such a poor and inconsequential city bore the grandiose title of Emperor instead of King.

It seemed that some centuries ago, when Ning became populous and sizable enough to require a firm central rule, the chief elders and tradesmen of the city approached the wealthiest of the Ningivite merchants and offered him the kingship. This individual, one Shub the First, adamantly refused to accept the crown, acidly pointing out that the title of "King of Ning" was an absurdity, due to the unfortunate rhyme.

Every royal court for thirty kingdoms around, he claimed, would find irrepressible humor in the term, and scurrilous jokes would soon be circulating which would render forever ridiculous the Ningivite monarchy. No such unhappy similarity of sound, however, accompanied the title of Emperor, and so this alternative was agreed upon and the first of the Ningivite Emperors was crowned.

The Wild Girl could see no point to this rambling

anecdote; however, she was clever enough to understand that her new master simply liked to talk to any available audience, so she made no protest. The meal itself occupied her fullest attentions, for she had not eaten so delectable a repast in all of her fifteen years, and she gorged herself gluttonously. I fear she also tackled the wine goblet a bit to excess, either because so fine a vintage had never before caressed her gullet, or because she was enchanted to observe how, once emptied, her chalice was instantly replenished by invisible hands. At any rate she drained the lees a half-dozen times, as if to observe this small miracle in repetition.

The meal concluded, it was time for rest. The Wizard again snapped his fingers and the unappetizing pile of sour-smelling straw was transformed to a sumptuous four-poster with a luxuriously deep mattress and any number of plump soft pillows. Giggling, the Wild Girl peeled off the Wizard's best robe and, bare as an eel, bounced up and down on the bed. And when at length they retired, the Wizard was rather pleasantly surprised when his companion was the one to initiate some further activities. The girl, in fact, was rather surprised to find herself making overtures, but doubtless the cause lay with the surfeit of good wine she had imbibed.

At any rate, the Wizard acquitted himself heroically, despite his wobbling paunch and advanced years, and later, cozy and warm and relaxed, hovering on the twilit borders of sleep, Ooo drowsily decided that being owned by a fat green Wizard was not such a bad prospect after all. His ingenious athletics, and his staying power, caused her to compare him not unfavorably with a champion of the tribe, much admired by those of her comrades in nubility, a youth with the rather apt and appropriate name of Hung. Moreover, the Wizard was gentle, considerate, and kindly in Bed. She fell asleep richly satisfied.

The Wizard, gazing down with affectionate humor at the tousled, gently snoring girl, heaved a sigh, wished he were one or two millennia younger, and dozed off himself.

2.

Concerning a Rather Unorthodox Mode of Leaving a City in Haste, and How Ooo Learned Her New Master's Name and Began to Entertain Suspicions About His Motive

The sun-star Kyliz was well up into the morning sky before the Wizard roused himself from bed, and he would probably have snoozed quite a bit longer had his repose not been interrupted by a natural need to which magicians are no less vulnerable than are ordinary mortals.

The cracked jug, however, was somewhat lacking as a sanitary facility. So the Wizard transformed it as he had earlier transformed the table and the bed. From her cozy nest of blankets, Ooo stared in awe at the marble bathtub, the gleaming alabaster conveniences, the sparkling knobs of solid gold, all of which melted out of thin air upon command.

Once the call of nature had been answered, and while luxuriating in a steaming tub full of sweet-smelling pink suds, the Wizard tutored his new *chela* in the use of such niceties. Accustomed from infancy to nothing more sophisticated than a latrine trench and a muddy river full of corkodrills, the Wild Girl delighted in the oils, perfumes, unguents and rosewater, to say nothing of the luxury of hot and cold running water. But she had to be instructed to flush the commode after use, and she shudderingly scorned the notion of immersing her entire body in the bathtub. Bathing, to Wild Girls, is an occasional need, not a pleasure.

The Wizard shrugged affably. "As you will, my dear *chela*," he said. "If being dirty pleases you, then by all means be dirty. There are few enough ways in this world for people to assert their individual natures."

She giggled, wrinkling up her nose. "You talk funny," the girl observed. Then, "What's a *chela*?" she asked.

"A magician's servant, pupil, companion, and, in certain cases, bedmate," he replied absently, being then engaged in conjuring up their breakfast.

The sweet-smelling pink suds after all tempting her curiosity, Ooo dipped wriggling toes in the tub and eventually, and timidly immersed herself therein. She splashed about a bit, sneezing when the soapsuds got up her nose; on the whole, however, she rather enjoyed the experience of bathing. At very least, there were no corkodrills to watch out for—these being mean, toothy saurians like alligators which infested the muddy rivers of her homeland and whose infestation, rather naturally, made bathing infrequent as well as considerably hazardous.

"You had best stop splashing about and come to breakfast," the Wizard observed, "before your breakfast gets cold."

"What's 'breakfast?' " the girl inquired.

"A morning meal. One of the more enjoyable amenities of civilization, rather like bathrooms. Oh, remind me to make the bathroom disappear, will you? If I forget, the innkeeper will have a fit when he sees it. And, for all I know, that cracked jug may be a family heirloom."

The Wild Girl came padding over to investigate breakfast, wearing nothing but a towel wrapped around her wet hair. She giggled again at the unfamiliar sensation of being "clean all over," and turned about in a small circle with her arms raised above her head, calling the Wizard's attention to how clean she was. Casting a judicious glance over the sleek, wet, glistening, and still somewhat soapy expanse of girlflesh, he murmured a word or two of praise and, with a friendly pat on her bare posterior, bade her pitch in before he ate it all himself.

"These are scrambled ahuti* eggs," he remarked

* The ahuti is an interesting sort of bird whose main claim to fame is that it feeds on nothing at all material, but is nourished by the wind itself. Other such birds with the same peculiar

around a cheekful of the same. "And we have griddle-cakes with melted butter and yuggleberry syrup, hot muffins with four kinds of jam, cold wineapple juice and a pot of cocoa. Eat up now, for we must be gone from here rather quickly. But do try these sausages!"

Ooo began eating, eyeing him curiously. It was obvious she had a question to ask, but it was quite some time before she had downed her first few mouthfuls and was able to ask it.

"Why we have to go so quick?" was the question, when she finally got it out.

"Because," said the Wizard, buttering another muffin, "when I purchased you last night, I forgot to make the transformation of pebbles into *pazools* permanent. And in thirty minutes the slave master will be here with two of the civic guards to demand my arrest for counterfeiting, or something. And you will end up back in the slave pens, probably no worse off than you were before I came along, but certainly no better."

Then he winced and said in a slightly pained voice, "Please *chew* before swallowing, my dear *chela*! We are not in *that* much of a hurry."

Turning everything back into whatever it had been originally—including the bathroom—and causing the scanty remnants of their breakfast to dissolve again into their component elements, took virtually no time at all.

Ooo was, I think, rather understandingly reluctant to cover up her bare, beautiful, and thoroughly clean young self in the Wizard's best red robe and pouted for some time when he firmly insisted.

Having paid for the night's lodgings in advance, they had no reason to leave the inn by the front door, especially since the irate slave master and two bored guards were just then entering The Full Belly, even as the Wizard had predicted that they would. So the Wizard and his *chela* went down the back stairs, out through the kitchens, obtained the fat scarlet lizard

---

diet are the gouith and the alphalim. The discerning reader will, ere long, discover that every bird, beast, reptile, fish and tree in this book is completely fabulous or legendary, and none of them has been invented by the author. An amusing notion, I think.

from his stall, tipped the grimy stable boy, and departed the premises by means of the back alley.

As there was only room in the saddle for one, the Wizard either had to let Ooo ride on his lap, or expect her to trot along behind. On the whole he preferred the lap idea and had no reason to regret his decision, as the Wild Girl proved a cuddly lapful.

Ooo, however, was filled with curiosity about everything in sight and asked many questions. She had never seen a city before—not that Ning was much of a city, of course—and wanted to know what everything was for. When the Wizard, in mild exasperation, inquired, she informed him that she had been sold to a passing slave caravan in order to settle her father's debt to the local purveyor of fermented beverages, and had only entered the gates of Ning yesterday morning. When you are packed like sardines in a covered wain with thirty-six other slaves, you have little opportunity to see the sights, she pointed out rather tartly. Except, of course, that she used a ruder simile than "sardines."

"Oh, very well, then," he said. "To reply to your forty-ninth question since leaving, that peculiar 'hut' with the human faces all over it is the Temple of Aboom the Avaricious."

Ooo wrinkled her nose up at the name, which she didn't dare try to pronounce. "Who is *that*?" she asked with a grin.

The Wizard stifled a groan, this being the fiftieth question she had asked in ten minutes. "The God in His Aspect as Patron of Pawnbrokers, Misers, Usurers, and All Bankers," he explained, rather shortly. This was the third temple they had passed since leaving the inn, and he rather thought Ooo should be able to spot them for herself by this time.

"Who is this 'The God' you keep talking about?" she inquired pertly. The Wizard blinked, giving her a look of mild astonishment.

"Good heavens, my dear, don't they worship The God where you come from?" he demanded.

"Nope," she said positively. "Wild Folks don't have no temples." She went on to explain that her tribe worshipped—or, at any rate tried to keep on the good side of—the Rain Demon, the Storm Sprite, and a malevolent trio of genii called the Wugglux to whom were attributed all toothaches, rheumatism, fevers, night-sweats, bad dreams, snakebite and cases of hemorrhoids, impotence and female complaint.

The Wizard rolled his eyes up piously at such heretical goings-on, and observed that a Prophet should be dispatched to the Barbarian Mountains beyond the trackless plains of Chun, and the sooner the better. He then elucidated the Mysteries to the girl, explaining that Zao, as any enlightened planet should, observed the tenets of a strict monotheism, although for practical reasons The God was separately celebrated in each of His ninety-nine principal Aspects, a total which included the sum of every legitimate human profession, craft, or means of employment. They rode on thereafter in silence for a while. But not for very long.

Counterfeiting, in Ning, is a capital crime—which is only to be expected in a state which chronically exists on the verge of bankruptcy. And the fuming and furious Zool had succeeded in prevailing upon the local magistrates to close all four of the city gates against the possible escape of the Wizard and his purloined, or at least unpaid-for, slave girl. Even now, squadrons of the civic guard were combing the inns and caravanserais of Ning in hot pursuit of the culprits.

It could have been a sticky predicament, had not the Wizard been a wizard. But—as we already know—he was.

Once it was clear that the gates were closed and closely guarded, the Wizard simply reined his waddling steed off the main thoroughfare and into a side street. Six or seven minutes later this street debouched against the city wall, the row of houses which had lined it to either side lapsing into a huddle of squalid huts built right up against the purple wall.

"What we do now—fly over?" Ooo asked apprehensively.

"Not," remarked her master, "while I am still digesting my breakfast." And blinking amiably about, he informed the wall in mild tones of unmistakable authority that it no longer existed.

And, of course, it didn't. And the hovels which had leaned against it collapsed, no longer having anything to lean against. While the girl stared at the immense opening in the wall with a stunned expression on her face, the former inhabitants of the now-flattened hovels set up such a squawk of lament and outrage that the Wizard had to scoop up a handful of pebbles and turn them into gold *pazools*—thoughtfully remembering just in time to make the transformation a permanent one—and toss the coins to the loudly complaining gaggle of crones, shrews, oafs and urchins, to mollify their outrage. He then rode through the opening in the wall out into the open country, closing it up behind him again.

The slave girl, still not quite accustomed to such displays of magic, sat on his lap in stunned and slack-jawed silence for a while. Then she turned about and asked him—it was a reasonable question, given the circumstances—that if he could make the city wall vanish into thin air, wouldn't it have been a lot simpler to have paid the slave master in regular, or at any rate permanent, coin?

He considered the point for a time, then smiled.

"I suppose, on the whole, that you are right, my dear *chela*. On the other hand, I have always had a weakness for spectacular magical effects, and, as it happens, I have never before had the occasion to depart from a city in quite so sensational a manner, and thought it would be a pleasure. After all, what's the good of being a magician if you can't have a little fun working magic once in a while? As Quluk the Loquacious, a philosopher quite highly reputed over in the Land of Lu, has pointed out in his admirable *Maxims for Magicians*, 'A feat a day keeps boredom away.' And in his *Commentaries on Quluk*, the celebrated Mung observes that magic is like a muscle: to keep your powers in trim they must be exercised frequently. I have always thought, myself—ah?"

The girl was examining him with a slight but unmistakable frown on her features.

"You," she remarked, "talk too much."

"Umm," said the Wizard, lapsing lamely into silence which persisted for quite some time.

They had by this time crossed a stretch of sandy desert whose monotony was relieved at intervals by stony outcroppings and the occasional clump of witch-broom whose prickly stems and thorny, scraggling branches afforded little pleasure to the eye and absolutely no relief from the scorching sun-star, by this time well up in the sky.

Before noon, however, they reached a narrow, muddy river which they waded across at the nearest ford. On the farther side the country became a mite greener: graceful feathery trees appeared on the horizon, flowering bushes clothed the slopes of low hummocky hills. A trifle after noon they came to a large stand of trees perched beside a picturesque small lake of cold, indigo water.

Here they paused for lunch and a nap. For some reason not caring to conjure the meal into being, the Wizard, lolling comfortably upon a blanket spread out beneath the nearest tree, instructed his *chela*, in her capacity as servant, to pick two of the large, round rubbery yellow leaves from the tree. These were as large and as round as dishes.

This done, the Wizard unlimbered a fishing pole, a line and a hook, and proceeded to go fishing while the *chela*, still serving in the same capacity, hunted firewood and built a small fire. The Wizard proved to be an angler of remarkable skill and in no time two plump fish were sizzling on the spit the girl had rigged.

While the fish were cooking, the Wizard employed his *chela* in her capacity as bedmate, putting the blanket to good use. Obviously, riding so many miles with a curvaceous, and now sweetly scented, Wild Girl on one's lap tends to whet other appetites than merely a desire for lunch.

They dined happily on crisp, delicious fish steaks spread out on the dish-leaves. The Wizard produced salt and pepper shakers from his saddlebags, together with a fat black jug filled with a green, syrupy liqueur that tasted interestingly of mint. After lunch it was time for a brief nap. When they awoke, Kylix was well down the slope of the sky and the afternoon was well advanced. Ooo was snuggled cozily up against him, naked as a blade of grass, playing idly with his queue and looking coy and kittenish.

"What's on your mind?" he inquired idly. For reply, she snuggled closer.

"D'you s'pose we could try that last one again?" she whispered.

He looked at the position of the sun-star, and noted the length of the tree shadows. "I don't see why not," he smiled. "We have a half an hour to kill, although we must be—somewhere else—in two hours and twenty minutes."

"Why?"

"Because we must meet someone at that time," he replied. "Come here, my dear."

"Who we gotta meet?" she persisted, ungrammatically.

"*Have to* meet," he corrected absently. "You'll see: now be a good girl and come here. No more questions."

After they had tried that last one for a while, discovering it to be strenuous, but certainly not impossible and really quite rewarding, the Wizard returned to his blanket for a brief snooze. But Ooo lay awake for a while, wondering to herself how the Wizard could possibly know what was going to happen before it happened. *Nobody* knew that, as she was well aware: but her Master obviously did, for he had known just when to attend the slave market in order to buy her before the buyer for the palace harem arrived.

It was all very curious, thought the Wild Girl to herself. And she began to wonder just why it had been important to her Master to buy her. Why *her*, when any girl would do—and there had been some real beauties among the merchandise.

Ooo had never considered herself to be of any particular importance to anyone save herself. Now it seemed she was, at least to the fat green magician who lay at her side on his back, snoring softly.

It was all quite odd.

At about the time when the Wizard had, perhaps carelessly, predicted they would meet "somebody," the fat puffing lizard breasted a steep hill, and there below them was a caravan of gypsies.

The gypsies had drawn their dilapidated caravan of wagons up by the shore of a shallow, muddy-looking river, had unhitched their steeds from the wagons, and were letting them drink at the river's edge. The steeds in question were not, of course, horses, this being the planet Zao and not the planet Earth. Instead, they were yales—four-legged creatures about the size of horses, but covered all over with spots, with little curling pig's tails, and a set of movable antlers on their heads. The yales snorted, smelling the approach of strangers, and showed their teeth in the strangers' direction. The teeth were imposingly long, and finished off with two curling boar's tusks, one to each side of the mouth.

Nodding complacently to himself, and wearing the slight, satisfied smirk of one who has reason to congratulate himself upon being proven correct in some prediction or other, the Wizard gazed down at the gypsies. Then he thumped his heels in the lizard's ribs—it puffed out its scarlet throat indignantly at this familiarity—and they went waddling and slipping and sliding down the slope and into the valley, through whose midst the river meandered.

The gypsies watched them come, idly, exchanging eloquent bright-eyed glances and uttering occasional chuckles. The sight of a wizard on a lizard was a new one to them, obviously. But they saw nothing about him or his companion at all to arouse their apprehensions.

The gypsies were tall, strapping men with gleaming ebon hair, glowing red cheeks, bright black eyes, and remarkably white teeth. They wore suede leggings and voluminous sashes of vermilion and velvet trousers of bottle green and embroidered snake-skin boots. They also wore gold hoops in their ears and necklaces of gold and silver coins and far too many jeweled rings on their fingers. They grinned a lot, Ooo noticed; and they looked her over appraisingly, which she also noticed and didn't much like. Especially since she had forgotten or neglected to put her robe back on after lunch and what had followed.

While the lizard, hissing with mortification, was wading across the shallow river, the Wizard smiled expansively, and waved a leisurely hello to the gypsies. They didn't look any too happy at his approach, since he was obviously a magician of some kind or other and they *can* be troublesome, if not treated right. They put their hands casually to their waists, where a great many dirks, daggers, stilettoes and other assorted cutlery were sheathed, scabbarded or tucked, and watched him come with doubtful eyes.

The gypsy chieftain came out of his wagon, shouldering aside dangling pots and pans which clanked and clattered, to take a long, shrewd, suspicious look at the fat green man on the fat red lizard. This personage was old and lean and leathery, with waxed fantastic moustachios so elaborately curled and trained that Ooo, muffling a giggle, wondered if he had to sleep standing up leaning with his back to a tree to avoid messing them up.

As the Wizard rode into the caravan, the gypsy chief strutted forward showing all of his teeth, in a display of dental splendor doubtlessly to be interpreted as a smile of welcome. The teeth in question all had prominent gold fillings, and the fillings themselves were set with rubies, sapphires, emeralds, and at least three blue-white diamonds. It was, taken all in all, quite a smile.

"What can the Haxar Nation do for you and your lady, *huzoor?*" the chief inquired at the termination of a bow so low and so eloquent with flourishes that Ooo half expected him to fall on his face in the mud. This did not happen.

"I have a morsel of information which you very much desire—or will desire—to possess," said the Wizard lazily, taking a swig from the fat black jug of green liqueur. "In payment for which, I will take off your hands that funny-looking parrot in the bird cage on the fourth-wagon-from-the-end."

The chief exchanged long, cunning, puzzled looks with his men. These swaggering braves came a bit nearer, their beringed hands still very close to the hilts of their many knives. From the look in their eyes, Ooo guessed they were wondering if magicians bled blood like other people.

"The fowl in question, *huzoor*, is of a breed so rare as to be fabulous, and worth an inestimable price in the bazaars of the city of Droob," remarked the gypsy chief.

"Not if you never get to the city of Droob," pointed out the Wizard.

The chief regarded him with mystification and a definite unease. Wizards were chancy folk, easy to offend, difficult to get rid of, and remarkably ready to turn harmless and inoffensive folks into purple toads if not handled with proper finesse. The chief looked at him again, and dubiously, guessing that he was being euchred but unable to do much of anything about it. It was obviously a situation new to his experience. He was used to euchring others—it was, after all, the gypsy way—but being himself euchred had at least the benefit of novelty. He essayed another glittering smile.

"The sun-star is hot, the road is wearisome. Why should we haggle, *huzoor*? Come—dismount—enjoy the hospitality of the Haxar Nation! Our wines are subtle and potent, our women beguiling and voluptuous. And we can always discuss the fowl in question when the appetites of the flesh have been sated with—"

"You have thirteen minutes," observed the Wizard tranquilly.

The chief, now distinctly unhappy, gnawed on his lips in a silent fury of frustration. At length, wearing a doleful expression, he bowed again.

"The fowl of your desire is your honorable property, *huzoo*," he growled between gritted teeth. "Gafredo, fetch the miserable creature—quickly."

The hooded cage securely fastened behind the saddlebags, the Haxar chief confronted the sleepy-eyed fat Wizard, arms akimbo, moustachios bristling with suppressed emotion.

"And now, *huzoo*, of courtesy, what is thees morsel of information that we so desire?" he hissed, eyes flashing.

Thumping his heels in the lizard's ribs and tugging the reins to head it about toward the river again, the Wizard nodded carelessly back over his shoulder.

"Firedrake," he said with admirable brevity. "Be here seven minutes from now. It's best you were on the other side of those trees by the time he arrives."

While the lizard clawed and scrambled back up the slope of the hills, having crossed the shallow river, the Wizard removed the cloth covering from the bird cage, revealing a most unusual looking bird. His feathers were bronze, copper-green, peacock-blue and of purest gold. His head was scarlet, trimmed with indigo, and his eyes were like wise black jewels.

He was, as the Wizard later explained to Ooo, a simurgh.

But the most astounding thing about the simurgh proved to be neither his appearance nor the fact that he was, actually, a simurgh. It came to Ooo's attention when the bird cocked a bad-tempered eye at the smirk on the Wizard's fat green face and uttered a disgusted noise, and said in a sharp, clipped, metallic, but perfectly understandable voice, "So it's you again, is it, Oolb Votz, you old rascal?"

At which the Wild Girl almost fainted. Recovering herself a bit dizzily, she said, "Oolb Votz? Is *that* your name?"

"It is," he acknowledged, taking another swig of the green brandy. "But you should call me 'Master.' "

They had gotten over the crest of the hills by this time and the lizard came to a halt, panting furiously, on a ledge. Just then something went roaring and hissing and screaming past down the length of the river. A sultry orange light flashed through the crevices between the hill peaks, followed by a scorching hot wind like the breath of a blast furnace. Hissing and squalling, it faded in the distance and was gone.

The gypsy caravan had, of course, made for the farther hills with every conceivable haste the moment that the Wizard had informed them just what was impending. So—happily for the gypsies, but perhaps unhappily for the firedrake, who presumably had a taste for such two-legged morsels—they escaped its passing unscathed.

When the sultry breath of the monster's meteoric passage eased, a ringing silence ensued.

The Wizard took a squint at the sun-star, and nodded with satisfaction.

"Right on time," he remarked with a grin. "Not bad, not bad at all—in fact, really quite commendable! Firedrakes are usually such unreliable creatures, you know, and simply have *no* sense of time at all."

The lizard puffed and wheezed, but said nothing in response to this astonishing statement, perhaps because it was not able to speak. The simurgh, who was, also didn't.

And as for Ooo, she made no response either, having just fainted dead away.

3.

Concerning a Loquacious Simurgh, Several Music-Loving Troglodytes, and a Rather Persistent Dragon

Talking birds were another new experience for Ooo—every bit as quaint and curious as bathrooms, and quite a lot more interesting. The Wizard roused her from her faint with a liberal prescription of the minty green liquor from his seemingly inexhaustible black jug, and as they proceeded on their way to wherever it was that they were going, the Wild Girl regarded the bird with considerable curiosity.

Oolb Votz had said they were on their way to meet someone. Ooo wondered if this was the someone in question. So she asked the befeathered individual, who ruffled up his neck feathers with asperity.

"I certainly *am* Someone, my dear young savage!" the bird replied pertly. "You, on the other hand, are no one in particular. But, as the only true, genuine, warranted simurgh currently in existence upon this planet, I am a celebrity of considerable note, mentioned in all of the more elegant mythologies, and with a not-inconsiderable position in several of the better bestiaries. Hmmph! What impertinence! 'Are you someone?' Indeed!"

The Wizard chuckled but said nothing.

"Then," persisted his *chela*, "what's a simurgh?"

"A member of the winged species *avian simurghi*," sniffed the simurgh. "Easy to identify because of his gorgeous plumage, ready wit, intelligent conversation, amiable disposition, and fabulous abilities."

Ooo giggled, but presented a straight face when the bird glared at her.

"What abilities are those?" she inquired presently.

"Well, longevity, for one," the bird explained. "Like my cousin the phoenix, I am exceptionally long-lived. But unlike that relative I am under no necessity to renew my term of existence by periodic self-immolations. No, indeed! When The God molded me from the primal dust—or from whatever residuum remained after He had divided the primordial *ylem* into the several elements whereof matter is composed—it pleased Him to indulge in a whim for immortality denied to the more ordinary creatures."

The bird had begun his disquisition huffily enough, but his sharp temper soon lapsed into a good-natured loquaciousness. It is difficult to be in a bad humor when you are invited to talk about yourself, and before long his mien was really quite amiable. And besides, the Wild Girl listened attentively without any signs of losing interest—unlike most people to whom the simurgh talked for any long period of time. He began to regard her almost fondly.

He explained that on the ninth day after the creation of Zao, the Divinity, having by then established the firmament and divided the dry land from the midst of the waters and shaped the Moon and quite a number of small, frivolous clouds, and played a bit by turning the sunsets off and on, had begun to experiment with inventing life.

His first experiments in this area had resulted in two great beasts, the leviathan, which lived in the seas, and the behemoth which inhabited the land surface of the nine-day-old planet. The trouble with these creatures was, while they were certainly novel in their appearance and of an imposing size (each being as large as your common or garden mountain range), they were simply too cumbersome for the element in which they found themselves. The behemoth, who weighed something in the neighborhood of thirteen million tons, rather evenly distributed on his eleven legs, was so heavy that he caused an earthquake every time he shifted his weight from one set of feet to the other. And the leviathan was so large that she displaced millions of tons of water, and before long it was difficult if not impossible to tell the dry land from the seas. And also, The God had forgotten to create anything for these first two beasts to eat.

So (explained the simurgh) the Divinity, with a sigh, scrapped His first experiments and began all over again. This time He invented much smaller creatures, much lighter in weight, but no less novel and interesting. First he made the catobleps and the su and the lamussa and the tchataka bird who quenches his thirst only from the raindrops and the hydrus and the imdugud and the nyaggle and the boyg, not to mention the aquqim and the gouith, a kind of bird without any legs who flies about all the time and is nourished by the wind itself.

Warming to His task, and with (as the simurgh affably pointed out) that superior artistry that experience gains for any artist, He then created the simurgh and the leucrocotta, the arandus and the enfield, the phoenix and the babwyn, to say nothing of the manti-chore, the shiqq, the yetl and the copard phalmant.

"I was created immediately after the tarandus, as I recall," the bird reminisced dreamily. "A beautiful creature, the tarandus—it was the color of opals, as I recall—and I remember gazing at its several shifting hues with considerable pleasure and even delight. Of course, it wasn't a bird, you know— But then, I am quite satisfied with my own colors, which, if less various than that of the tarandus, are at least stationary and permanent."

"And what did He make next?" asked Ooo, who found the legend quite entrancing. Since nobody had ever told her any stories before, she would most likely have found any legend equally entertaining: nevertheless, she was quite enjoying this one.

"I believe it was the physeter or perhaps the rosmarin," the bird mused. "Unless the sadhuzag and the zaratan were next. There were ever so many of us, you see, that it shortly became rather difficult to keep all of the different names in mind. Now that I think of it, it must have been the pastinaca, because it became somewhat over-excited by the sheer experience of actually existing and caused the most frightful stench. We always had that trouble with the pastinaca—not that it could help it, poor thing!"

After listening to an account of the subsequent creation of thirty-two more creatures (none of whom she had ever heard of before), Ooo became just a trifle restive. As if sensing the inattention of his audience, the simurgh went on to skip the next few days of creation, during which the waff, the porphyrus, the yazata, the senad and the tragelaphus,* and several more creatures with even curiouser names and natures, took shape. The loquacious fowl thereupon expanded a bit upon his account of the experiences of the earliest of living creatures upon this planet.

"Well, sir, the trouble turned out to be simply this," the simurgh explained. "In the first place, each one of us was a pure and distinct individual, you understand, without any particular gender. The God had not, as yet, really thought through the question of sex in all its ramifications, you see, and it had not as yet occurred to Him that in order to reproduce, we would require females of our own kind. But after he had created the androsphinx, as I recall it, He thought a moment or two, and then summoned into being the gynosphinx: that, of course, is why the Mountains of Thu, to say nothing of the Sung Plateau and the Hills of Vak, and quite a large portion of the Desolation of Eryx, are to this day so thickly infested with sphinxes.

"By then, you see—or rather you probably *don't* see, for I really do not quite understand it myself—it was somehow too late to go back and create female partners for the rest of us. I've never been exactly clear on this point. Perhaps The God was too bored with the idea of repeating all of those early creations of His . . . or maybe (for all I know!) He had forgotten exactly how He had done us up the first time around . . . but, anyway, and whatever the reasons were, He made none of us with female companions. To sort of make up for it, I assume, He went back and made us all immortal—well, most of us, anyway, because by that time the

* Please see my previous footnote concerning the fabulous and/or legendary nature of the flora and fauna of Zao. I repeat: I really did not make up any of these creatures—no, not even the nyaggle, the babwyn, the shiqq, the yetl, or the waff. They are to be found in several of the better and more inclusive dictionaries of fabulous beasts, although a few of them have heretofore eluded the researchers of such texts.

manticore had devoured the senaps and was about to make a snack of the enfield, while aspidochelone had polished off the rosmarin and would have made short work of the hippocamp had not the remora held him firmly in his tracks, as it were. . . ."

Unable to understand that last bit, Ooo wrinkled up her small, pert, adorably freckled nose. The Wizard, who had been lazily half listening to this account (having perhaps already heard it all before, during his earlier association with the simurgh), yawned and cleared his throat.

"Aspidochelone was a giant sea creature," he said, "sort of like an enormous turtle. So big that sailors were always landing on his shell, thinking it an island. I believe the dear fellow still haunts the waters down south around the Isles of Ix. Anyway, the remora is a very small, feeble-looking little fish with remarkable powers of suction. If he determines to do so, he can stop a ship dead in the water just by anchoring his tail about a rock and sucking on the hull. Peculiar little rascal!"

"Quite so," nodded the simurgh. "I have always considered the remora an example of the Divinity's sense of humor."

By this time they had come quite a way, for the loquacious simurgh was a slow conversationalist who frequently wandered astray from his subject into the interesting side paths of diversion, and he could not resist a quaint anecdote, even where such were not strictly relevant to the topic at hand. The fat, waddling lizard was by now panting furiously and quite out of breath. Spying a small pool which flowed out of an aperture in the low, rocky hills just ahead, he flopped about and made for this oasis, ignoring the wishes of his master. They had to clamber off his back rather quickly, or be immersed. Indeed, Ooo only just retrieved the saddlebags and blankets in the proverbial nick of time.

The Wizard sat down under a manzanilla tree and took another swig from his bottomless black bottle, while Ooo stretched and gazed about interestedly. They had come into a rocky and desolate-seeming country that looked rather discouragingly as though it might decide to become a desert just a little way farther on. Ooo asked about that, and the Wizard nodded sleepily.

"It will indeed, my dear *chela*, in another half-mile or so. The Desolation of Yu they call it hereabouts, as I recall. All of the deserts in this continent are called 'Desolations' for some reason or other. A fancy of the map-makers, perhaps. Lends your ordinary, everyday desert a touch of class and distinction, I would say."

He was about to say something else, it being his feeling that the talkative simurgh had monopolized the conversation quite enough that afternoon, when a peculiar visage peered fearfully timidly at them over the crest of the small rocky hill directly behind the pool in which the lizard was, at that precise moment, floating on its back with all four, short, fat legs sticking up into the air.

Ooo saw it, too, and uttered a surprised squeal. The face popped down out of sight behind the rocks at this piercing sound. It had been rather an odd face, at that, with fat cheeks, small weak eyes, enormous flapping ears, and a long fat nose which distinctly resembled an elephant's trunk.*

"You needn't be alarmed, my dear," said Oolb Votz. "They are quite harmless, and are really more afraid of you than you are of them. Timid creatures—ungainly, but gentle."

The head had emerged into view again, and was now joined by two others. One had an iron ring in its ear and might just possibly have been considered female.

"What *are* they?" whispered Ooo, trying not to stare.

"Troglodytes, of course," said the Wizard, waving at them in friendly fashion. "I had forgotten a tribe of them had taken up residence hereabouts recently."

* A minor example of the author's thoughtfulness toward his readers. Books of this nature partake of an element of translation: there being no elephants extant upon the planet Zao, this comparison could never have occurred to my characters. They would have thought the organ in question resembled the proboscis of an enfield. There are, however, no enfields alive on earth any more—if, indeed, there ever were—so I have modified the term for my reader's benefit. The skills involved in this kind of work require considerable forethought. I just wanted to point this out in case you thought I was getting careless.

"What are Trog-trog—whatever it was you said?"

"Troglodytes are human enough in their way, but prefer to live in underground homes because the light of the sun-star is too bright and fierce for their eyes, which are small and very feeble. They are shy creatures, but not unfriendly and even hospitable, or so I have known them to be if treated properly. Perhaps we shall be invited to dinner, if we play our cards right."

The Wizard dug through his baggage, producing a small flute upon which he began tootling. These pleasant warblings made mild, gentle music which went nicely with the lavender shadows of twilight and the first few faint stars. A mild breeze rattled sleepily in the leaves of the manzanilla tree (in whose boughs the simurgh sat, head under respendent wing, snatching a brief nap). Presently, the timid Troglodytes came forth to listen.

"They are very fond of music," the Wizard observed. "Perhaps because their ears are so large, and they hear it better than we do. Or maybe it is because they so seldom get to hear any."

He tootled on, and before long more Troglodytes came forth from their burrows to squat at a safe distance from these interesting strangers and to enjoy the flute music. Their huge elephant ears swayed in the breeze, flapping forward to catch the tones of the flute. From time to time they looked shyly at each other, smiling faintly. Ooo found them quite interesting, and not at all frightening, for they did indeed seem harmless—like innocent, stumbling clumsy-footed babies, for all that they were a good seven feet tall. They had large, clumsy hands and feet and wore no clothing at all, their bodies being colored all over a sort of grayish-purple, like a plum. She was amused to notice, as they edged a bit nearer, that, for all their size, their sexual parts were as small and undeveloped as little children's.

The sun-star Kylix sank from view behind the hills, painting the cloudless skies lovely shades of tangerine and purest gold, which gradually deepened to crimson and royal purple. The stars came forth upon the night-dark heavens in glittering multitudes, like the jewels of many empresses. The Wizard played on until it was really too dark to see. Then, wiping the flute's mouthpiece against the hem of his robe, and stowing it away in the luggage again, he directed Ooo to go and see if the Troglodytes had left them anything by way of thanks.

They had, indeed. Fresh, ripe melons, ground-nuts, milk-bearing pods not unlike our coconuts, and several hollow gourds filled with a succulent, steaming meat stew, as well as a copious (and quite tasty) green salad of tender shoots, diced tubers, and wry, mouth-puckering yellow berries. The salad came neatly wrapped in large rubbery green leaves. Waking the simurgh, they dined sumptuously around a small, crackling fire made by magic. The lizard, disdaining such fare, went rooting for grubs and worms and ant eggs among the roots of the tree, and may be presumed to have made a hearty repast.

Ooo was ravenous, as usual, and ate everything in front of her, taking particular delight in the meat stew. The Wizard idly debated with himself whether or not to inform her that the Troglodytes, among their various unsavory habits, took pleasure in the meat of serpents, scorpions and a kind of giant earthworm that grew twelve inches thick and two hundred feet long, and that such subterranean dainties were undoubtedly represented in the stew.

He decided to do the kind thing, and held his tongue.

After dinner, wrapped in blankets and staring up at the stars, Ooo asked him why he had bothered to entertain the timid Troglodytes rather than making their meal by a spell, as he had done back at the caravanserai.

"There's only so much magic in the world, why should I use it up if I don't have to?" he asked rhetorically. "Besides, I enjoy playing the flute, and it gave pleasure to the Troglodytes, who have few enough pleasures, poor creatures! Then again," he added around a yawn, "it's fun to sing for your supper once in a while."

The next day they continued in their meandering and apparently goal-less journey, and the Desolation did in fact decide before long to turn itself into a decent, self-respecting desert—complete with scorpions the size of fairly large dogs, and rather more prickly cactus than anybody could possibly have wanted to see.

They had gotten halfway down into a particularly rocky and dusty and unpleasant gulley when it became obvious to them all that larger and even less pleasant forms of life shared the Desolation of Yu.

It went flapping by overhead with a rush and a hiss and a whiff of fire and brimstone, darkening the sky and casting a shadow distinctly dragonish in outline. Ooo at first thought it was the firedrake come back again, weary of hunting the gypsies, but it wasn't.

It was definitely a dragon.

When the lizard clambered up out of the gulley they had the opportunity to take a good, long look at it, for it was negotiating the middle atmosphere at an elevation of about a quarter of a mile. It flew in large, lazy, aimless circles, remaining in view at all times, and such was the crystalline clarity of the dry, clear desert air that the monster could be seen in its every revolting detail.

It had a long snaky neck, armed along the top part with a jagged ridge. And an ugly, wedge-shaped head with cold, burning green eyes that blazed from under scowling brows. Its jaw resembled that of a corkodrill's, but it had ever so many more teeth, and on the whole they were longer and wickeder, and not only did they lend the monster an appearance that was sinister, but also one that looked distinctly *hungry*.

Its four crooked legs were armed with dreadful bird claws like the talons of some enormous beast of prey, and its tail was long and sinuous and wriggly, and was tipped with a barb which looked exactly like an arrowhead. It had big black ragged wings like a bat—but a bat the size of a locomotive.

Oh, it was a dragon, all right. No question about that. Ooo had never seen one before, but that made no difference. When you actually do finally see a dragon, you *know* its a dragon.

From time to time, from flaring nostrils, it emitted a long *whoosh* of snapping orange flames, which terminated in a puff of dirty black smoke.

"It does that because it's hungry," the Wizard remarked. "The reptile has gas, you know, just as we do. When we are very hungry and our tummies are empty, they rumble sometimes from the gas, which is rather impolite, I suppose, but very human. The dragon has exactly the same condition: but in *his* case, the gas is quite flammable (or do I mean *in*flammable, I always get the two words confused: one of them means it can be set on fire, and the other means it is fireproof—inflammable *ought* to mean fireproof, at least it sounds that way to me, but I have a feeling it's actually the other way around—)"

Just then the Wizard went diving off the back of the lizard, and rolled under a prickly cactus with such haste that he did not even bother to finish his parentheses. So did they all, in fact, except for the fat red lizard, who drew in his feet beneath himself, and tucked his head back, rather like a turtle. And the simurgh, who launched himself into startled flight with a shrill, indignant squawk.

Because, just then, the dragon came zooming down at them like a dive-bomber, jetting flame and looking hungrier than ever.

He veered away sharply, banked, and climbed into the middle atmosphere again, obviously deterred by the cactus—for not even dragons enjoy getting cozy with a prickly cactus, and you may be very certain that the Wizard had chosen one with remarkably long, sharp, wicked-looking spines to hide under.

It came circling back, looking down at them with that very direct and unmistakable expression on its face that people get when they are looking at their lunch. Seen from up close, it had scales only on its back, and they were a dirty, muddy-green color, and the size of dinner plates. The rest of its long, wriggly body was covered with a tough, leather-looking hide, all pebbly and rough, colored a dark green, gray-green, turning yellowy toward the underneath parts.

It whooshed fire at them again.

"As I was saying, before I was so *rudely* interrupted, the stomach gas ignites when they burp it out, because of an enzyme produced by glands situated just behind the third row of teeth," the Wizard said. He was trying to sound calm, but it came out just a bit breathless and somewhat indistinct. This may have been because his mouth was full of sand at the time.

"Make it go away," said Ooo faintly. "Do some magic or something!"

"*Ahem!* It—ah—isn't quite as simple as all that, my dear," the Wizard said feebly.

"Why not?" demanded Ooo, not unreasonably. "You're magic, aren't you?"

"Yes, I am," said Oolb Votz, with dignity. "But, then, so are dragons, I'm afraid. Their magical powers are not inconsiderable, as the better fairy tales and mythological epics amply demonstrate. And when one magic creature attempts to do magic on another magic creature, well, the results are indifferent at best, and sometimes downright dangerous. It tends to short-circuit the whole thing, if you know what I mean. Do you remember the story of the Magician Oop? Oop attempted to transform a witch named Oog into a purple toad. At the same time, Oog was working a spell upon Oop—or trying to, anyway. She was trying to turn him into a blue worm. Well, they both blew their fuses or whatever-you-want-to-call-it (there is a professional terminology for this sort of thing, but you wouldn't understand it). And when the dust cleared, Oop was worm from the hips down, while Oog was toad from the hips up. Neither of them was particularly pleased by the results, but I have always thought that Oog got the worst of the deal—"

"Are you just going to lie there talking, without doing anything?" cried Ooo as the dragon came by, skimming the rocks, trying to burn them out from under the cacti with its built-in flame thrower. "This dragon isn't going to be scared away by talk, you know."

"Um, I believe you are right, my dear," said the Wizard faintly. "It does seem to be a rather persistent brute. Hunger can give one an ugly temper, and as I seem to recall, dragons only eat about once every lustrum—that means every five years. I should imagine you could build up quite an appetite in five years. . . ."

He craned his neck and peered about. The dragon was circling overhead, preparing to make another pass. His last fly-by had burnt the tops off of the cacti. Another pass or two, and he would be all set to come flapping down to dine on roast Wizard and broiled Ooo.

The Wizard looked distinctly unhappy. He also looked quite blank. He knew he was supposed to do something, but, to be honest, he didn't have the slightest idea *what.*

"Here he comes again," groaned Ooo. "Play your flute at him, or something!"

"Dragons are really not all that fond of music, I'm afraid," said the Wizard distractedly. He was snapping his fingers and patting the ground in front of him, and mumbling something under his breath that sounded rather like a child's skip-rope rhyme—never having skipped rope, Ooo couldn't quite be sure. She had a dreadful feeling in the pit of her stomach that the Wizard had suddenly lost his wits. In fact, she asked him if he had.

"One, two, three, four,
Blow, wind, Rain, pour;
Five, six, seven, eight,
Atmospheric moisture—precipitate."

Having mumbled that, he broke off long enough to snap at her, really quite short-temperedly: "Do be quiet for a moment, girl, I am trying to conjure up a rainstorm!"

"Why?" demanded Ooo, beginning to lose her temper.

"Drat it, girl, because dragons hate them like poison. Gets their wings wet—the membrane soaks up water like canvas—and, also, it can extinguish their breath. Puts out their fire, in words of (mostly) one syllable. They can't fly and they can't go *whoosh*. They usually crawl under a rock and sulk until it's stopped raining. Now *do* be still and let me get on with it, will you?"

Ooo subsided, smiling happily. A raindrop had just struck her on the back of her neck.

II.

THE SIMURGH AND THE SHEBITES

4.

Discusses the Consequences of Rainmaking, the Persistence of Dragons, and Some Unexpected Aspects of Theology

"I am *not* complaining, mind you," the simurgh was saying in a grumpy, peevish tone of voice a while later, "I was merely pointing out that when one must tamper with the forces of nature, it is better to err on the side of caution and of prudence, than to be too liberal."

Neither Ooo nor the Wizard bothered to reply to this, being, the both of them, much too sodden and drippy to feel like arguing. The rain had been pouring down for the better part of an hour by this time, and showed absolutely no signs of lessening. Of the adventurers, only the fat scarlet lizard seemed to be enjoying the deluge: he tended to stop and to splash happily in puddles, whenever he came to one, which was rather often. As for Oolb Votz and his curvaceous *chela,* they were long since soaked to the skin and could have gotten no wetter had they for some reason tried. Actually, the simurgh, whose feathery plumage was protected by certain oils, was the driest of them all, and the most comfortable (not counting the lizard). Which was why Ooo thought to herself, rather miserably, that it was unfair to the bird to complain so much. And, after all, the rainstorm the Wizard had conjured up had accomplished its purpose in driving away the dragon.

The Wizard was riding along slumped over moodily, with the cowl of his robe pulled up over his bald head as far as it would go, saying nothing but prudently taking aboard frequent dollops of the mint-green brandy from his bottomless bottle as a precaution again the ague, the rheumatics, and the sniffles. From time to time he passed the bottle back to the Wild Girl, who was riding behind him.

Seeing that his plaints no longer drew any response from the pair of sodden humans, the simurgh, who was riding along perched atop the lizard's head, heaved a bitter sigh and contemplated the turgid heavens with what may accurately be described as a jaundiced eye. Never particularly fond of wet weather even under the best of circumstances, he had earlier prefaced his soliloquy on the dangers of magic-making with the remark that he figured he had, by now, had enough rain to last him for at least the next millennium, give or take a century or two. It occurred to him now to expand upon this observation, as a few choice elaborations on the theme presented themselves to his fancy. A glance at the doleful visage of Oolb Votz, however, made him wisely decide to hold his tongue for once: the expression on the Wizard's sad green face rather suggested that he might inwardly be meditating on the taste of simurgh stew. Such was, in fact, the case.

They continued plodding along from puddle to puddle, there being nothing else to do. The landscape which stretched away to every side was flat as a pancake, and very nearly as soggy. Not a tree, not a hill, not a bush or a ravine appeared in view to afford the slightest shelter from the drizzle. The Wizard might have conjured up a brace of umbrellas, had it not been for the unfortunate fact that these useful appurtenances had not yet been invented on the planet Zao. So they rode along, wet, cold, miserable, and gloomy.

An hour or so later, however, the downpour began to lessen and light could be discerned breaking through the interstices of the clouds. The shower died to a drizzle, then dwindled to an occasional drip-drip-drip.

"About time, too," wheezed the simurgh with grumpy satisfaction. "I will never understand the ways of magicians! How one may have the power to start it raining, yet at the same time be unable to stop it from raining when one wants no more, escapes me—"

"Oh, stop complaining, you bothersome bird!" sighed

Oolb Votz, dismounting squishily and beginning to squeeze the water out of the hem of his robe. "It is hazardous enough to rearrange the climatic and meteorological conditions of half a continent in order to produce a required precipitation; the cessation of such does put rather a strain on the weather. And if you don't believe *me*, remember what happened to the cities of Rux and Zoar when Soob the Sorcerer attempted to turn off the east wind he had summoned for the Emperor's regatta. I refer, of course, to the Great Hurricane of '02."

"Do you think you could make a fire?" asked Ooo timidly. "Then we could dry off real nice!"

"Not a bad idea, my dear," Oolb Votz observed, and he promptly conjured up a stack of dry, neatly-piled firewood and a large cardboard box of kitchen matches.* In no time they were basking before a merry, crackling fire, feeling much drier and ever so much more cheerful. Especially as the Wizard had thoughtfully provided them all with shish kebabs on silver skewers, bread and butter, and mugs of hot cocoa topped with whipped cream* all around.

After the snack, they snuggled cozily together, letting their eyelids droop, feeling warm and sleepy and comfortable, as people usually do when they are digesting something hot and yummy. That goes for simurghs, too.

"Where are we heading, Oolb Votz, if you don't mind my asking?" inquired the simurgh a while later. "Not that I am not duly grateful for being rescued from those tiresome gypsies, of course; but I can't help wondering as to your plans. Since the last time I accompanied you on one of these expeditions—that fatiguing sea voyage to the Isles of Wuk-wuk, what with all of those Blue Savages and the various assorted

* Well, not exactly: remember what I said in my footnote in the previous canto? What he did get was a *zabberwij*, which is the Zaoic equivalent of a tinderbox, or flint-and-steel, or something. Please, from here on, keep clearly in mind my observations on the translating of exotic terms into familiar equivalents, for I simply cannot continue interrupting the smooth flow of my narrative for these bothersome footnotes.

* See my last footnote. I am not going to remind you again.

jungle fauna (almost every variety of which seemed to have a highly cultivated appetite for simurgh, if not, indeed, for Fat Wizard!), and I have *never* been able to understand why you required those Ninety Fire-Pearls anyway, which occasioned the adventure! Well, needless to say, I entertain certain trepidations, not to say apprehensions, at the notion of assisting you in another of your perilous and crack-brained projects."

"You should never," observed the Wizard lazily, "open a clause unless you are capable of finishing it. Elementary grammar, my dear fellow! However—and I will charitably ignore that indignant snort as being beneath my dignity to notice—we are wending our weary way through the waste, going nowhere very much in particular, and merely permitting adventures to happen to us, as hapless travelers must. This life, my dear bird, consists of a haphazard sequence of accidental meetings and partings, very few of which can ever be anticipated, avoided or fully understood. The element of sheer Chance, my friend, conflicting as it does with the first principles of Causation, denies any premeditated plan on the part of Destiny. Destiny, therefore, may only be defined as the sum total of one's accumulated experiences, which are themselves accidental and purposeless. 'Purpose,' you deduce from this, is an interpretation imposed upon a sequence of events *after the fact*. Recall, my dear chap, the amusing accident which occurred to the Philosopher Quung, while strolling, deep in thought, through the Summer Garden of the Winter Palace! He slipped upon the skin of a fruit and fell, as the saying goes, flat upon his face. What was the *purpose* for which The God placed that fruit skin in the path of the estimable Quung? 'No purpose at all,' you say. 'It was sheer accident!' And, of course, you would be correct in so remarking. But the fact of falling upon his face when his feet slipped out from under him caused the Philosopher to deduce the existence of the Force of Fallation, a mystical and up-to-that-point unsuspected natural property inherent in all material objects to *fall downward* unless otherwise supported! This is rightly deemed one of the triumphs of Human Reason, and a landmark in the history of

Natural Science. In this regard, then, the 'purpose' for which The God situated that greasy bit of fruit skin in the path of the preoccupied Quung was in order that the existence of the Force of Fallation should be realized by Mankind. This is a *post-facto* interpretation, of course, and the better logicians, I suspect, prefer to argue from *a priori* evidence, but still, and on the whole—!"

"You talk too much," observed the simurgh tartly.

"Um," said the Wizard.

And, "That dragon is coming again," said Ooo, wearily.

"The persistence of dragons has been previously noted in the better class of bestiaries," puffed Oolb Votz as they were underway again. "Nikkidik, I believe, recalled a dragon over in Ja-Ja that pursued a flock of ahuti birds fully sixteen thousand *parasangs* before wearying of the chase, which had by then occupied his attentions for eighty-two days. And the sagacious Fungo records an instance when a party of pilgrims bound for the Oracle of Igg were followed across the desert by a tenacious dragon for two and a half months. (It must have been a member of some other variety of dragon than ours, of course—ours being your common or garden *Draco volans*, the 'flying kind,' you know—or it would have overtaken them quite early on.)"

"This," said the simurgh through gritted teeth—if simurghs *have* teeth, that is, a question on which I hold no certain opinion—"is a time for *more* magic, and *less* talk!"

"But no more rain, please!" wailed Ooo.

Twilight had fallen a little while before, and the keen eyes of the Wild Girl had observed the approaching of their scaly bane through an odd, intermittent orange-reddish glow on the horizon to the south, which soon turned out to be the dragon's panting breath, when observed under conditions of darkness. The determined reptile was indeed still pursuing them, and now that its wings had dried out again, it had made rather excellent time.

"Oh, no, that would be contrary to the Laws of Nature," said Oolb Votz in shocked tones. "That—*ahem!*—slight cloudburst I occasioned earlier in the day has quite exhausted the moisture contained under current atmospheric conditions. We shall have to think of something else—"

And he went fishing through the saddlebags, emerging at last therefrom with a fat, greasy little book of magic spells and remedies he carried with him as a rule. Thumbing rapidly through the pages (which were covered with minute characters, written in red, green, purple, crimson and gold inks, with occasional drawings of talismans, amulets, periapts, sigils, horoscopes, pentacles, and various cabalistic symbols), he began mumbling under his breath, "*Drama,* Rules Of . . . *Dramazod* (See under *Zaazonash*) . . . *Dreams,* Interpretation Of . . . *Dropsy,* Cure For . . . *Dwarves,* How To Get Along With . . . *Duchiel,* Invocations To—Oh, dear, I am looking in the wrong direction!—Dragons . . . Dragons . . . Ah, here we are! Hm, now let me see . . ."

But before he found another remedy, a walled city had appeared out of the murk and the lizard, who needed no other prompting, having a well-developed sense of survival, made for it in all haste.

They reached the gates just before they closed at sundown.

Even the hungriest of dragons, it seems, hesitates to take on an entire city, so the disappointed reptile swung away and headed for the Land of Wuz, thereon to vent his rage in what the Wuzites were ever after to recall as "The Year the Dragons Were So Bad."

Ooo had enjoyed, as yet, very little experience with cities, but even when you take into consideration the limited exposure she had enjoyed to urban conditions, it was obvious to the Wild Girl that one city is really very much like another one. Or, as she would put it, When you've seen one city, you've seen 'em all.

This particular city, for instance, had a stone wall around it, just like Ning, and here and there they had cut a gateway through the wall so that people could come in and go out whenever they wanted to. The only difference that she could see between this one and the other one, was that Ning had been mostly purple, while this one was, for the most part, red.

And it had streets of bumpy cobblestones that meandered between twin rows of top-heavy wood-and-plaster houses, whose second stories hung out over the first floor, and the usual variety of inns, wine shops, temples, caravanserais, stables, smithies, palaces, mansions, warehouses, whorehouses, dens of thieves, dens of iniquity, antique shops, grocery stores, slave markets, meat markets, ironmongeries, potters' shops, this kind of shops and that kind of shops, and so on.

The populace seemed to be composed of beggars, urchins, priests, panderers, policemen, thieves, blacksmiths, horse trainers, horse traders, lepers, slaves, wealthy persons, the nobility, magistrates, bums, cutpurses, winos, streetwalkers, men selling parrots, men selling sweets, men selling brassware, men selling their sisters, and more priests. There seemed, in fact, to be an awful lot of priests. Some of them wore yellow robes and some wore black robes, and more than a few of them were in surplices of white or gray or brown or even lavender.

There also seemed to be an awful lot of temples, which probably explained all of those priests.

The Wizard set up shop on a street corner directly in front of an inn called The Stuffed Turkey, and proceeded to do tricks for the crowd while his *chela* passed the hat at intervals, the idea being in this fashion to procure a sufficiency of the local currency to pay for their night's lodgings. The Wizard flatly refused to turn any more pebbles into *pazools*, having learned his lesson back in Ning. "If one doesn't learn from one's unhappy experiences," he wisely observed, "what's the point of all that suffering?"

His *chela* noticed that the sort of magic he was doing was of the sleight-of-hand variety. While amusing the gawking yokels with his display of prestidigination, he kept up a running patter which went something like this:

"The name's Mugwump the Mysterious, folks,

former Court Enchanter to His Majesty, King Oj of Zotz . . . Watch closely now, my dear friends . . . Nothing up my sleeve . . . *Hey, Presto!* There you are, madam, a red top for your adorable little boy . . . What's that you say, sir? All done with mirrors, you say? . . . *Slam-bam, Alicazoo!* I pluck a fresh egg from your ear thusly, a white pebble from your left nostril . . . Yessir, folks, As Performed Before The Crowned Heads of Yurp . . . Never before seen in these parts . . . Little trick I learned during my lengthy visit to the Robed Sorcerers of Bungo . . . Yes, from the Grand Master himself . . . Now, watch carefully, my dear friends . . . The hand is quicker than the eye!"

Ooo peered into the hat, discovering two slugs, one washer from an old faucet, a flat round stone, and a copper penny, the last of which she bit between her strong white teeth. (It bent, being made out of tin painted copper color.) A nudge in the Wizard's ribs and a nod to the hatful suggested that a somewhat more sophisticated brand of thaumaturgy might be required, if they were not to dine on what the garbage in the alley contained, and spend that night in a doorway.

The Wizard sighed, and plucked a bright red seed from thin air. In impressive silence he dug a small hole in the mud with the toe of his slipper, dropped the seed therein, smoothed the mud back over the small depression, and tucked his hands into the voluminous sleeves of his robe, closing his eyes until he looked positively Buddhalike, and maintained a complete silence while a small green tendril squirmed up out of the muck, became hairy, sprouted other tendrils which thickened, climbed, grew, thickened some more, became man-tall, taller, even taller than that, thrust forth branches, grew scabrous with bark, leafed, flowers budded, blossomed, produced fruit which fattened, rounded, reddened into ripeness.

While the leaves withered and dropped one by one, and the bark crumbled, and the branches withered, shrunk, fell off, and the trunk flaked visibly away, eventually becoming a rotten stump which fell to powder and vanished, the Wizard, having plucked one of the riper fruit, thoughtfully skinned it and ate it, all but one bright red seed which he returned to the thin air from which he had gotten it.

Considered all in all, it was quite a trick.

And it got him arrested.

About midnight the simurgh finally located Ooo huddled in a doorway looking hungry (which she was), and cold (she was that, too), and scared (no question on that one, either). She was gratifyingly glad to see him.

"Should have inquired as to the name of this dump," grouched the bird sourly. "Forbidden City of Sheb, they call it. Run by a bunch of priests—whachamacallit—a theocracy."

"But why did they arrest him?" whimpered Ooo. "He didn't do anything. Nothing that he doesn't do all the time, anyway!"

"Didn't *do* anything, you say?" snarled the bird—and if you have never happened to hear a bird snarl, let me advise you that it will raise your hair—"He created a tree out of thin air, didn't he? Have you got any idea how that sort of thing looks to a bunch of priests, my dear young woman? Like anathema, that's how: like blasphemy. They got him in the slammer on a charge of Heresy in the First Degree, and I, for one, am perfectly willing to let the old fool stay there until Ginungagap freezes over!"

"What's that?"

"What's what—Heresy or Ginungagap?"

"Heresy."

The bird shrugged, ruffling his bronze-and-peacock-blue plumage.

"Theology has never been high on my list of favorite subjects, to say the least, but I *think* it means boiling in oil, followed by a bit of drawing and quartering, and if any of you is left when they're finished, you get smeared with molasses and buried up to your chin in an anthill. Oh, do stop that whimpering, I didn't really mean it . . . there, there, girly . . . it isn't as bad as all that."

After a while, the simurgh got Ooo to stop crying, and explained that the creating of a tree out of thin air was looked upon as something of a major misdemeanor by the city fathers here in Sheb, since it tended to infringe upon the prerogatives of the Creator. Oolb Votz had been hauled up before the Grand Inquisitor and was condemned for Sorcery, Vagrancy, Heresy and Mopery in less than half an hour. He now languished in a cell high in the Tower of Pain, such being the delightfully apt name of the church prison.

Sheb being a theocracy was naturally ruled by the priests, and priests are naturally bigoted in favor of their own narrow creed, and intolerant of differences of opinion on theological matters. It's really too bad that things are that way, but there you are: you have to take a world the way it is, not the way you would prefer it to be. And the priests of Sheb, who had a law against virtually everything that was any fun to do, like rape, seduction, public drunkenness, cheating on your income-tax returns, blowing up banks, incest, assassinating public officials, playing with yourself, and smoking Happyweed, also had laws against the practice of the Art Sorcerous.

"But what are they *doing* to him?" Ooo whimpered.

"Well, nothing right now. The Inquisitors have the weekend off, for religious duties, and the Torturers are temporarily on strike for higher fringe benefits," explained the simurgh. "When I left, the fat old fool was playing chess with his guards and getting drunk on the contents of that little black jug of his, and talking away as if the night would last forever. It infuriates me, when people can't take seriously their own impending dismemberment, to say nothing of boilings in oil and the anthill!—Just kidding!" he hastened to add as Ooo began to snuffle again.

The bird explained how he had come to learn of these matters. The simurgh, who looks to be nothing more than merely a rather flamboyantly colored fowl when he manages to keep his mouth shut, had fluttered around the eaves and window ledges and courtyards of the Hierarchial Palace, listening at windows, peering in through the shutters, and, in general, keeping his ears and eyes open.

By managing to overhear snatches of conversation between the various Deacons, Vergers, Sextons, Lay Brothers, Nuns, Priests, Monks, Lamas, Bonzes, Cardinals, Bishops, Arch-Episcopals and Mother Superiors, and by putting two and two together—coming up with "four," in the approved tradition—he had learned the Wizard's sentence and his current place of imprisonment. The condemned man, he remarked grumpily, had been served a hearty supper, and when last seen was suffering no particular pain. Indeed, he had thus far beaten the turnkey three games out of four.

"But what are we going to do?" whimpered Ooo.

"Well—"

"We've got to do *something!*"

"I know, but—"

"We've got to save him! We just can't sit around and let those horrid priests do those terrible things to him."

"You are right, of course, but still, it's, well, not quite as simple as all that—"

"What are we going to *do?*"

The simurgh cleared his throat, and looked around helplessly. The night was dark and moonless and the sky was streaked with clouds, through whose rents Olymbris shone as a golden spark and Gulzund as a spark of white, and Thoorana as a spark of dim red flame. Zephrondus had, as yet, not risen above the horizon.*

The night was therefore dark, and, as the streets of Sheb the Forbidden City were not illuminated, and as most of the people of the city were in their beds by this hour, they were deserted.

"Well?" demanded Ooo.

The simurgh cleared his throat a little, but said nothing.

"What are we going to do to save him?" the Wild Girl demanded tearfully.

There was quite a long silence.

Finally: "I don't know," the bird admitted gently.

And neither of them had anything to say for a long time after that.

* These, with Zao itself, are the five planets in the solar system of the star Kylix.

5.

In Which the Wild Girl Proves Sharp-Witted, the Simurgh is Demonstrated to be Resourceful, and the Hero of Our Story is Discovered to be Quite Drunk

In the end, it was Ooo who came up with the answer to the problem. It was really quite a simple answer—but then, the problem itself was none too difficult, when you stop to think about it. Nor did it prove particularly difficult to persuade the simurgh to give it a try, for that remarkable fowl was really quite fond of Oolb Votz, and, after all, owed it to the Wizard to return the favor he had done the bird by releasing it from the bird cage in which the gypsies had imprisoned it, by springing Oolb from his own durance vile.

Entering the church prison was as easy as the proverbial pie, for windows are seldom locked above the first floor of a building, it being a widely accepted fact that very few burglars can fly. But simurghs are exceedingly adept at the art of aerial navigation, and before very long this particular specimen found a half-open window and vanished therein, swallowed up by darkness.

The bird had no very clear idea precisely where, in this ecclesiastical slammer, the keys to the cells would be kept. But he had a feeling that whoever was in charge of the various heretics, blasphemers, and other offenders against Holy Law, would probably keep the keys close by him. And this particular individual would probably be the Grand Inquisitor himself, a scrawny old geezer with a long nose, quite red at the tip, and sharp, hard, unfriendly eyes which bore a close resemblance to the ends of two steel gimlets.

Hopping into the corridor, the resourceful fowl proceeded to find the bedroom of the Grand Inquisitor by the simple process of searching for it. It seemed likely to the clever bird that the Inquisitor would live here in the prison, where all of the cells and dungeons and torture chambers were, if only to be close to his holy work. Luckily, at this hour of the night everyone within the citadel was either in bed or standing duty at his guard post, and the upper levels of the building were deserted, at least the hallways and the stairs were, anyway. So the simurgh encountered no opposition while giving the prison a good search.

He found the Inquisitor's bedroom with hardly any trouble at all: assuming that it would be the most luxuriously comfortable room in the place, he turned in at a doorway sumptuously hung with velvet drapes and odorously redolent of myrrh and frankincense. A night-light flickered smokily before a holy icon depicting several of the more anatomically ingenious of the torments of hell. By its wan but persistent luminance, the sharp eyes of the inquisitive fowl discovered the Grand Inquisitor himself. This distinguished personage was in a large and comfortable bed, full of plump cushions and draped with satin sheets, with a woollen nightcap adorning his bald pate, hands folded piously upon his bony chest, snoring lustily.

On a bedside stand the bird immediately discovered a large key ring containing quite a large number of keys, which reposed atop a handsomely illustrated volume of ribald tales which the Inquisitor had been perusing before retiring to his slumbers. It was but the work of a moment for the simurgh to flutter up to the top of the stand, and to flutter down again, holding the key ring against his feathery breast in one tight claw so that the jingle of loose metal might not arouse the Inquisitor from the arms of Morpheus.

If locating the keys had been simplicity itself, it proved somewhat more tiresome and difficult for the simurgh to locate the cell in which the Wizard was immured. There were so very many cells, you see, filled with moaning wretches, and he must peer into each one in order to ascertain whether or not Oolb Votz might not also lie within. He had already managed to locate the Wizard's cell from the outside of the prison, of course, but once within the immense structure his orientation went awry and he became quite confused, what with the meandering passageways and the endless corridors lined with cells, which went every which way.

At length, he identified the cell the Wizard was in through the obvious expedient of listening for the sound of his voice. The bird well knew that, unless actually dead—or sound asleep—the Wizard would most likely be talking. And so, indeed, he was. His audience, at this late hour, consisted of a nervous young curate who, unable to sleep, had come down to discuss with the notorious Votz the salvation of his soul. Chasing off the turnkey with a shrill curse (for the curate considered games of chance, even such games requiring skill as chess, to be the Devil's playground), he was now sitting on the end of the Wizard's bunk, looking distinctly ill at ease. For the Wizard, nothing loath, had invited him in with hearty good nature, and had embarked upon a discussion of theology which all but stood the poor curate's hair on end. For it is bad enough, for the godly, to contemplate the abominable sins of heretics: it proved much worse to actually have to *listen* to one for more than half an hour.

The Wizard, you see, had listened good-naturedly to the curate for a while, but then began discussing the origin and nature and derivation of several of the theological points the curate had attempted to make. The notion that heresy is a crime of the soul, to be cured by the chastisement of the body, he pointed out in his amiable way, contained an essential error. For the soul has no real connection to the body, merely residing therein for the while. To punish the body for the sins of the soul was, therefore, about as irrational as to burn down a tenement building because it had temporarily housed a criminal. Far better and more logical, he suggested, to inflict pain upon the soul itself, by way of punishment. And, since the performance of sins are painful and unpleasant to the souls of men, which partake of the perfection of Divinity, the most acute punishment which might be inflicted upon the soul would be to force it into heretical error. In other words, as the curate soon realized, with blood-curdling horror, the Wizard was making the powerfully logical argument, that the best way to punish a heretic would be to insist that he persevere in his heresy!

The Wizard, having made his point, had passed on from the specific to the general, and was engaged in a lazy monologue on Comparative Theology as the simurgh reached his cell and peered in through the bars. He was, at that moment, expanding on the so-called Romanticist school of thought, a theory which accounted for the existence of the world in the system of the Arch-Heretic, Glugg.

". . . This interesting, and, if I may venture the opinion, novel doctrine, offers the notion that the entire world is nothing more than a work of romantic fiction being imagined by the brain of a fiction writer upon some higher Plane or Sphere. The Romancer, as Glugg terms the Demiurgos, is simply making it all up out of his own head, so to speak, and you and I and everyone else on Zao are in reality nothing more than figments of His imagination. We derive our own vitality, which is actually only an *illusion* of vitality, from the vigor and forcefulness of His gift for imaginative invention. Glugg, in his thirty-ninth treatise, speculates as to the *nature* of the literary work in question: that is, whether it is an epic or, just possibly, a tragedy—my own theory, by the by, is that we are all characters in a comedy of some sort, since it seems to me that, for the most part, life is more comical, more ludicrous, more—shall I say?—laughable, than it is heroic or tragic. —The Sonnambulist School, on the other hand, invented by Zunk the Blasphemer, presents the concept that the world is nothing more than a nightmare dreamed in the mind of a Madman on some superior level of being . . ."

The young curate, already pale to the lips, rolled his eyes up until only the whites showed, and began to pray in a trembling, feeble voice. Raised in an ecclesiastical society, where the tenets of the Faith are never argued, having long ago been all decided upon, he had never before been exposed to *any difference of opinion* on such holy matters. It was, indeed, for him an earth-shaking experience even to be listening to these hideous and pandemonial hallucinations, these nauseously original ideas, each one of which gnawed at the roots of his sanity like a voracious worm, until the poor fellow felt his reason began to totter and the foundations of his faith began to shudder and reel.

". . . Whereas, on the other hand, the ingenious Erg has promulgated a doctrine perhaps even more quaint, and his disciples belong to what they call the Nonestic School, derived from *non est*, which is to say, 'It does not exist.' Erg himself was one of the apostles of Thudd, who preached (as you may recall) that the world was in immediate danger of being destroyed by an irate and fed-up Divinity. The date of the predicted calamity passed without any singularly terminal convulsion of nature, and the Prophet Thudd promptly expired from disappointment. Well, the sagacious Erg postulated that The God had, indeed, destroyed the entirety of Zao, but the Evil Principle—largely, if I understand the Ergite hypothesis correctly, to invalidate Thuddism—in the very next instant, replaced the now-vaporized planet with an immense and complex illusion, or mirage. Therefore, as Erg would argue, neither we nor our world exist at all, but are part of a systematic delusion of the senses which manages to persuade our souls that everything has continued as normal, long after the disintegration of matter. Students of the Nonestic School, I understand, practice a mental discipline which encourages them to ignore the needs of the body and the realities of the world around them, and commonly expire of starvation rather early on, since to eat the nonexistent food which their nonexistent tummies require is to give tacit credence to the belief that both food and tummies do actually exist. . . ."

The curate by this time had both hands clapped over his ears and was on the verge of fainting. It was, then, only a blessed relief for the poor fellow when the cell door suddenly swung open, as if at the touch of an unseen hand, and a monstrous demon in the likeness of a gaudy and fantastical bird came flapping in, spouting a shrill stream of the most dreadful and fearsome and horrendous and mocking blasphemies.

He fainted dead away, with something of a sense of relief.

Along about dawn, the simurgh rejoined Ooo in the alleyway with the Wizard stumbling along in tow. It had not been very hard to get out of the Tower of Pain, after all. The front door had not even been locked, as things turned out—for, when you stop to think of it—why should it have been? Only a maniac or a fool attempts to *break into* a prison, and, this being the case, why bother with the door? And, as for the guards stationed in the cell blocks to prevent any of the whimpering wretches from making an escape, they were no less ignorant and superstitious than the curate had been, and the simurgh's impersonation of a demon was of a superior quality of convincing realism. (The simurgh had known more than a few demons, imps, succubi and evil spirits in its time, being a bird of catholic taste in acquaintances, and certainly knew how to act the part.)

The Wild Girl was so delighted to see the Wizard actually free again, and seemingly unharmed, that she threw herself into his arms, weeping hysterically, and covered his smiling and rather sleepy-looking face with kisses. He grinned, chuckled, mumbled something in an indistinct voice, and tried to pinch her small, rounded bottom, missed, and fell over and lay there laughing.

"Oh, what have they *done* to him?" wailed Ooo, clasping her hands against her palpitating, and deliciously plump, bosom.

"Nothing," said the Simurgh in a disgusted voice, "except to encourage him to stay up talking all night. The fat old fool talked so much he had to wet his whistle on the contents of the that fat black jug of his that never seems to be empty. By this time the old rogue is quite thoroughly liquored up, dang the luck!"

Ooo gasped, blinked, looked, looked again, and giggled.

For it was quite true: the Wizard was sound asleep

now, and snoring loudly, a blissful smile on his features. And drunk as drunk can be.

They got him on the lizard somehow, using straps from the saddlebags to tie him on top. And then they rested from their exertions, trying to figure out what to do next. In little or no time the curate would either recover, or be discovered, and the fact that the prize heretic had decamped to presumably more hospitable lodgings would become known. It would be best, they decided, if they could manage to be outside of the Forbidden City by the time these unhappy events occurred.

But this, of course, presented problems.

It was by this time very nearly dawn. As yet, the city slept and the streets were steeped in darkness, but before very much longer the Shebites would be up and bustling about the day's business.

And the gates of the city were, of course, closed and locked. This was always the custom with walled cities at night, and I, for one, have never quite understood why it should be. Either the City Fathers lock the gates at night to prevent people from getting in—but why on Zao should they?—or to prevent people from getting *out*. On the whole, the latter explanation seems to hold the most water; but I have never been very sure as to the reasoning involved.

However, the fact remained: the gates were locked and there was simply no way for Ooo and the simurgh and the lizard and the Wizard to get out before dawn.

Had not Oolb Votz imbibed so freely from his never-empty fat black jug of minty liqueur, he could probably have disassembled a stretch of the city wall into its component particles, as he did, you will remember, back at in Ning. But he was obviously in no condition to perform any thaumaturgies which might be considered at all taxing, no, not in his present inebriated state, certainly.

"Maybe we could take a room in the inn," suggested the simurgh reasonably. "It would likely be about the last thing the local authorities would expect us to do. They would, of course, reason that we had somehow fled the city after breaking himself, here, out of gaol. We could throw a cloak over him and pass him off, maybe, as your aged grandmother, down with the sleeping sickness and here to visit the shrines for a miraculous cure."

"Umm," said Ooo, dubiously.

"Do I detect a questioning tone in your voice?" inquired the bird tartly. "Which might imply that you find a flaw in my reasoning?" His voice rose to an irritable pitch at the end of the sentence, and Ooo attempted to placate him with a hasty, apologetic smile.

"It is just," she said, "that innkeepers seem to want their pay in advance."

"Umm," said the bird.

"At least, that was the way things were in the last inn we stayed at."

"Umm," the bird repeated.

"And we don't have any money to pay them with," she further explained, perhaps unnecessarily.

"You've made your point," admitted the bird, glumly.

"If he was awake, he could turn pebbles into *pazools*," the girl added. "I know, because I've seen him do it. He is really quite good at that one. I, ah, I don't suppose," she began, hesitantly, "I don't suppose *you* know enough magic to be able to—?"

"I'm afraid not," the bird said, ruffling up his feathers. Then an idea seemed to dawn upon him: he opened and shut his beak; his eyes widened. "Well, I'll be a cross-eyed turkey," he remarked in a strained tone. The girl looked at him inquiringly.

"It's nothing, my dear," the bird said. "There is something about you that makes one *think*. It's quite a unique gift, I believe. And rather refreshing. You wait here. I'll be back shortly."

And with that, the simurgh flew off, a ghostly, flapping shape winging up through the gloom.

By the time that the first trickle of dawn light came seeping across the rooftops, he returned, giving her a bit of a start when he settled on her forearm.

"Hoe ow oor ahn'," the bird said, a trifle indistinctly.

"I beg your pardon?" said Ooo, mystified.

The simurgh did something gingerly and complicated with his tongue and mouth and cheeks.

"I said, hold out your hand," he repeated.

She did so, whereupon the clever fowl spat out five gold *pazools* into her palm. They were rather damp and sticky, but in all other respects seemed perfectly legitimate.

"However did you manage to—"

"Let us converse later, in the comfort of our suite," the simurgh said, with a small, self-satisfied smirk. "Dawn is breaking, and we should see to the hiring of suitable accommodations in the nearest inn as quickly as ever we may. Before the guards are out tramping the streets, looking for us."

They found, with very little time spent in searching, an establishment called The Groaning Board, wherein accommodations quite suitable were procured without delay. Only a yawning tap boy was on duty in the wineshop, ready to quench the thirsts of any early-rising laborers who might chance to require hair-of-the-dog. He roused a husky stable boy, who carried "Ooo's grandmother" up to the room they had taken, and managed to scrape together a meager, cold supper from scraps in the pantry.

With the door latched, and a chairback wedged tightly under the knob, the Wild Girl and the simurgh relaxed and grinned at each other. The Wizard, still *non compos*, snored on a pallet in the corner. Ooo went to take a peek out the back window and saw the yawning stable boy leading the fat red lizard into a stall, and returned with a giggle of satisfaction to her share of the late-night (or early-morning) snack, which they both washed down with copious swigs from the never-empty black jug.

"*Now* will you tell me how you got the money?"

"Oh, it was nothing much. *Really*," the bird disclaimed, with a shrug of one claw. "As I discovered last night, trying to get in the prison to free our fat friend over there, people seldom lock second-story windows, and never lock ones on the third floor. Few burglars hereabouts can fly, I gather: but flying is, I think naturally, one of my talents."

"You mean you. . . ."

The bird shrugged again, obviously pleased with himself, but pretending modesty. "I flew in one of the windows of the inn and borrowed a few *pazools* from the purse of a sleeping merchant," he grinned. The girl laughed admiringly: and it was as simple as that!

Since both bird and girl had stayed up all night trying to help Oolb Votz, they retired as soon as they had finished their little meal. Ooo shucked off her robe and snuggled in next to the Wizard, while the simurgh flew up to perch on a convenient rafter. He put his head under his wing, as birds for some reason always do—although Nature has provided them, I feel comfortably certain, with perfectly adequate eyelids—and was soon as sound asleep as was Ooo herself.

It happily did not occur to either of them that, had the taproom boy been a little more alert or a trifle quicker on the uptake, he might have wondered where they could possibly have come from, at that hour of the night.

But he wasn't; and he didn't; and neither did they.

Later that morning a squad of soldiers knocked on the front door of the inn, and a lengthy palaver ensued between a sleepy innkeeper and a tense, jittery priest. Ooo was half awake, and could make out enough of the conversation to realize that the priest was inquiring after a bald, green heretic of the masculine gender, with sorcerous proclivities. The innkeeper showed him the register, which contained a scrawled notation to the effect that the last party to rent a room had been a devout young woman and a paralytic grandmother, here to tour the healing shrines.

The grandmother had been covered up, so none of the green portion of "her" anatomy had been displayed. Since the young woman had not been in the least green, the innkeeper was able to state most positively that the runaways were not in his hotel. The priest and the soldiers went away to search other caravanserais, and Ooo yawned, grinned with sleepy satisfaction, snuggled up against the fat Wizard, and returned to her dreams.

None of them awoke until noon, and when they did, the Wild Girl and the simurgh were well-rested and feeling fit, as presumably was the fat scarlet lizard in its stall in the stables.

Oolb Voltz, however, was ravenously hungry, and rather irritable, and headachy—the condition known commonly as a "hangover" would seem, therefrom, to be a universal complaint, known to humanoids on every world fortunate enough to possess the requisite technologies for the fermentation of beverages.

He listened grumpily to their delighted account of the cleverness wherewith they had procured his freedom and their safety, and was not unappreciative, although in no mood for giving fulsome expressions of his gratitude.

He suggested breakfast.

Since it would not be wise for him to show himself in the main room of the inn—it being thought by the management of the establishment that he was not only not green, not male, and not a Wizard, but instead an elderly grandmother down with the sleeping sickness, Ooo obliged by going down and ordering breakfast for the three of them.

Another taproom boy, not the same as had been on the early-morning shift, brought up two huge trays which he left at the door. Luckily, it did not seem to be customary here in Sheb for such service to be rewarded with a tip: otherwise, the simurgh would have had to go out on another aerial scrounging mission, this time in broad daylight.

The inn's idea of breakfast was substantial and hearty, and lent credence to its appellation. Here at The Groaning Board, it would seem the board did indeed groan beneath the weight of the meals served up. There were mugs of steaming hot cider, and bowls of warm milk, shredded wheat and melted butter, great slabs of cooked bacon, platters of fluffy biscuits to be devoured with butter pats, marmalade and/or pots of honey.

The bird and the Wild Girl pitched in with zeal and gusto—their rather skimpy late-night snack having only taken the edge off their appetites.

The Wizard also pitched in without further ado. But he pitched back out again just about as fast. Noticing that he was not eating—that he had, in fact, retired to the farthest corner of the room, near the window, as if for some reason he found even the odors of their breakfast unwelcome—Ooo asked (around a mouthful of piping hot, deliciously flaky biscuit dripping with honey and melted butter) if anything was the matter. In her way, which was the immemorial way of all women, it made her anxious and edgy when the menfolk refused to eat.

The Wizard said nothing, but maintained a dignified silence. The expression on his features was one of a pained disapproval, similar to that of a gentleman of the cloth when observing the young folks behaving like young folks. Ooo looked mystified.

The simurgh gave a cackle of laughter.

"Think nothing of it, girl," he chuckled. "I suspect himself drank so much last night that his stomach refused to take aboard any solid food." He then went on to explain to the Wild Girl that sometimes a night of steady imbibement of the fruit of the vine tends to result not only in an edgy temper and a bit of a headache, but in a queasy stomach, as well.

The Wizard affected to ignore this exchange, pretending to be absorbed in the view from his window. But he could not help but reflect a bit sourly on the unfortunate fact that few conditions in life are so excruciating as to possess a ferocious appetite, but have an upset tummy at one and the same time.

6.

How a Bit of Minor Thaumaturgy Enables Our Friends to Leave the Forbidden City, and a Rather Dim-Witted Desert Djinn Helps Them to Elude Pursuit

By the middle of that same afternoon, the Wizard having recovered both his internal stability and much of his accustomed good humor, it became time for the adventurers to consider a mode of shaking the dust of Sheb from their feet.

The reason for this was, quite simply, that every hour they continued their residence in the Forbidden City only tended to increase the dangers of discovery. For the priesthood were not at all being good sports about the escape of the heretic, and the house-to-house search continued with undiminished severity. In fact, if anything, the authorities had stepped up the proceedings to what might fairly be termed fever pitch. Squads of soldiery camped on every street corner, subjecting the passersby to a sharp and narrow scrutiny, and priests were to be seen everywhere.

"My children," the Wizard yawned comfortably, after the termination of a brief afternoon nap and a light meal had satisfied both his appetite and his irritability, "I would say that it is time for us to be gone. Let us leave Sheb behind, with nought but happy memories of our brief but not unmemorable visit here."

Ooo was relieved to see the Wizard very much himself again, and she and the simurgh agreed with him that the sooner they left the scarlet walls of Sheb behind them, the happier they both would be. So it was amicably decided, with no dissenting vote (except, of course, for the lizard, whose wishes were not consulted in the matter).

The travelers settled their bill with the innkeeper quickly and simply enough. Oolb Votz chuckled admiringly at the manner in which the quick-witted simurgh had arranged a down payment on their lodgings, but found, in settling the final account, no necessity in further encouraging the burglarious creature in his newfound life of crime. By the same simple expedient that he had employed heretofore, the Wizard pressed into service a few ordinary pebbles which were of no conceivable use to anyone, except possibly to small boys who might want to shy them at a nosy curate or something. A few mystic passes, a mumbled word or two in the language which the Wizard referred to as "High Magic," and new-minted *pazools* came into being and, as quickly, changed hands.

Of course, the guard on the gates of the city had been heavily reinforced, if not indeed quadrupled, in order that the infamous heretic might not find it too easy to leave the Forbidden City undetected. Some manner of ruse or subterfuge must be found to obfuscate their identities, and the Wizard, for reasons of his own, selected the time-honored method of disguise. Indeed, he seemed delighted at the prospect, and the more he considered the possibilities inherent in the scheme, the more enthusiastic he waxed over it. As for the simurgh, he snorted disgustedly, and made loud and caustic comments on the inappropriateness of such juvenile escapades to fat old men who ought, by this time, to know better.

Oolb Votz ignored this, his equanimity unruffled. But he *did* seem to view the fun of escaping from the scarlet city in disguise with a rather boyish zest and gusto.

This or that or the other mode of impersonation was suggested, argued for and against, and finally discarded as being either too uncomfortable or too ridiculous or too difficult or too dangerous. Finally, the Wizard fell back on the simple and obvious choice whereby the Wild Girl and the simurgh had gotten them into the hostelry the previous night. That is, the Wizard would be Ooo's paralytic old Granny and she his devout grand-offspring. As for the simurgh, he would play the role of the family's pet bird, a simple artifice which required nothing more difficult from him than merely to keep his mouth shut. Although an occasional innocent and insipid chirp, as the Wizard observed, would not be out of place.

The bird snorted and made a few disgusted comments under his breath. But he went along with the scheme.

A minor enchantment was quickly cast, and the fat, bald, green-skinned Wizard became a wrinkled, apple-cheeked, twinkly-eyed, toothless, snowy-haired old beldam. Another small gesture or two and the tousle-headed Wild Girl became a demure, innocuous young lady of prim and proper appearance. The roguish gleam in her eye faded to a dull glaze, and her tawny, lissom, plumply curvaceous young self smoothed out its various, and very interesting, ins and outs and became plain, gawky, colorless and uninteresting. By the time the diminutive enchantment had been cast there was nothing at all left about Ooo which could raise more than a yawn of boredom from the most hot-blooded roué.

The lizard, of course, remained a lizard and the simurgh a simurgh. Although, on second thought, Oolb Votz bleached out most of the exotic coloring from the fabulous fowl, and caused some of his more gorgeous plumes to disappear, as well as his glittering crest. He thereupon assumed the likeness of a dull, listless bird of average hue. As a slight afterthought, the Wizard caused him to be penned in a wicker cage.

The simurgh looked grumpy, but said nothing at these further indignities. No fool, he was practicing the difficult task of refraining from speech, and if his enchantment into a common house-bird proved not to be an irresistible provocation to vociferous complaint, obviously he could keep silent under any lesser stimulus.

They ambled out of the Forbidden City astride the scarlet lizard, attracting no undue attention. The guards at the gate were harried and jumpy, but scarcely bothered to notice them, although the priests newly stationed there gave them a keen going-over which made Ooo, despite her placid, cow-like demeanor, inwardly quite nervous. However, just as they were about to pass through the gates, an officious sub-deacon came bustling up with a crackling parchment document under one arm and a silver-gilt aspergillus under the other.

"What's all this-here, sonny?" screeched the Wizard in his guise of a grandmother. "More stuff-an'-nonsense, is it, hey, ter bother honest, decent folk with? If'n my grand-dotter, here, an' I, don't get a-goin' soon, we do be about ter miss the las' ferry boat across the Tsa—an' *thin* we 'ud be in a pretty pickle, fer sartain-sure!"

"Pray do not discommode yourself, my good woman," huffed the sub-deacon distractedly. "Captain, a late instruction from the Holy Office! As the escaped heretic stands condemned for the despicable practice of the Art Sorcerous, it is considered not impossible that the villain may have transformed his outer appearance into the simulacrum of another—an illusion which can easily be dispersed by the rigorous application of Holy Water, which I have here in this dispenser—"

"Here, now, hey!" protested the toothless old Granny in alarm, "yew don't be meanin' ter splash thet-thar stuff all over a decent, respectibble, God-fearin' old 'ummin like meself! Nosirree, sonny, not on the Widder Chu! Why, my gran-dotter brung me here in th' fust place ter get me over th' sleepin' sickness—which as bin done, thanks be ter Th' God! An' now dew yew be tellin' me ye aim ter give me there rheumatizz in my ol' bones, what wif splashin' water all over a body, an night a-comin' on, as hit is? It'll be ther rheumatizz fer shore, bless us all! What's a pore ol' widder-'ummin ivver done tew yew, sonny, yer Holiness I mean, that yew'd dew any sich a thang—"

These voluble expostulations (carried out, you will notice, with an admirable attention to appropriate dialect, even under the stress of the moment), however, proved of no avail. Gritting his teeth and trying to ignore the toothless old Granny's pleas, the sub-deacon aimed his aspergillus at the trio on the scarlet lizard—which was already underway, and had begun determinedly plodding and flopping along out through the gates—and let fly with a hearty splatter of enchantment-dissolving fluid.

Sizzle—POP—flash!

The guard captain gasped, turned the color of dirty milk, and fell over backward with a clatter of bronze armor.

The sub-deacon turned white as a newly starched surplice and fainted dead away.

Most of the guards, and all of the under-priests, raised an hysterical chorus of yelps and squawks, and took to their heels in all directions. Among the hubbub such terms as "Sorcery!" "Witchcraft!" and "Vile enchantment!" could be made out, but just barely.

For, with a sizzling flare of blue fire, and a spitting of long pink sparks, and a devastating whiff of brimstone and sulphur, the various small enchantments the Wizard had cast just a little while before, ceased and terminated abruptly, when splattered with Holy Water from the silver-gilt aspergillus.

Leaving a fat, bald, green-skinned Wizard on a scarlet lizard with a Wild Girl in a voluminous red robe, and a wisecracking and *obviously fabulous* simurgh!

The road which led out of this particular gate of the Forbidden City of Sheb (it was the South Gate, as it happened, not that it matters to the sense of my narrative at all, but just to keep the facts straight), the road which stretched before them, I repeat, was empty of travelers at this particular hour of the day, which was an advanced hour of the late afternoon. So the fat scarlet lizard encountered no particular obstacle in its path, and flopped and puffed along at the very top speed whereof it was capable. As for the three adventurers, they said nothing in particular—there really being nothing much to say, under the circumstances—but clung grimly to the saddle and tried to avoid taking backward glances over their shoulders to see if they were being pursued.

This is probably because they knew all too well that they were.

It was, after all, only going to be a brief matter of time before the Shebite constabulary recovered their wits, their morale, their esprit de corps, and whatever else they had lost when the enchantment broke before their astounded and horrified eyes in so spectacular, and, if I may say, so pyrotechnic, a manner; and took after them with zeal, and determination, and quite a few sharp and spiky weapons of bronze.

"It is at times like this," the Wizard remarked soberly, "that I begin to wish I had adopted a hippogriff or a wyvern, or something else with big strong wings, to ride upon, rather than this flat-footed lizard! It was," he said thoughtfully, after a moment or two of introspection, "probably mere vanity that prompted my choice. The contrast between his red hide and my own attractive apple-green complexion, you know—"

"I swear," choked the simurgh, "you will still be talking when they lower you into your grave. Which may not be at a date too far in the future, the way things look right now. Can't you do *anything* but gab, you lazy rascal?"

"Such as?" inquired the Wizard, affably, seeming in no wise put out of sorts by the simurgh's sharp tongue.

"Such as speeding along this plodding, plump reptile of yours!" snarled the bird. "A bit of magic, perhaps, would not be uncalled-for, under the present circumstances, which seem to me to verge upon emergency."

"Here they come," whimpered Ooo.

The Wizard and the simurgh looked back. And here, indeed, they came, a full squadron of them, mounted on fleet-footed yales. They wore corselets of bronze (the soldiers, I mean, not the yales, which wore nothing except for the spotted hides Nature had provided them with at birth), and spiked bronze helmets, and greaves, and flapping scarlet cloaks, and they carried pikes, spears, billhooks, scimitars, and a perfectly exorbitant number of knives, daggers, stilettoes and dirks.

They were not, however, coming along any too fast. And, come to think of it, they did not look any too pleased at this current assignment. In fact, if anything, they looked just a bit unhappy about the whole thing. A couple of officers were angrily waving them on with loud exhortations—from the rear of the squadron, which is where your prudent and promotion-minded officer usually prefers to remain*—but the soldiers themselves looked decidedly unimpressed, or hard of hearing. They seemed to get in one another's way a bit more often than might usually be the case, and a considerable number of them fell back because their steeds had developed a bad limp, or they had just discovered their helmets needed straightening or their saddle girths required tightening, or they had an annoying pebble in their shoe. More than a couple of the ones in the front pulled over to the side of the road to blow their noses or because they had just gotten something in their eyes, and these men, with commendable unselfishness, waved their comrades on while they tended to this or that or the other thing.

Those who were waved on into the forefront in this manner did not, apparently, wish to hog all of the glory, and, while not exactly spurring their steeds on full-tilt, tried to encourage their fellows in the rear ranks to assume their rightful place in the fore. Some of the soldiers, in fact, were so polite that they drew off the road so as not to block their friends' path.

So—what with one thing and another—the fat, puffing red lizard had reached the shore of the River Tsa and was waddling out into the mud and the reeds before the first of the soldiers caught up with it.

That first soldier—suddenly discovering that he *was* the first—went all over pale, and bent over to tighten his saddle straps, thus giving the next few of his comrades a chance to catch up with him. After all (the fellow probably reasoned), why should *he* grab the opportunity for glory, when his chums, buddies and pals were equally deserving of winning medals or being mentioned in the dispatches. So loose were his saddle straps, and so cautiously did the others guide the footsteps of their yales down the slope, that by the time the others had caught up to him, the Wizard and his party were out in the middle of the river—for, obviously de-

* Perhaps operating under the theory that the officer who remains in the *rear* of any warlike activity, instead of foolishly rushing up into the front lines, where people tend to get themselves killed rather often, is the one who is still around, and still alive, when the promotions are given out later.

ciding not to wait for the slow-moving ferry, Oolb Votz encouraged with kicks and curses his fat lizard to swim across to the other side.

Luckily, the lizard was of an aquatic species, or at least an amphibian. Anyway, they got across the river, leaving the soldiers lined up on the other side. Their officers, still prudently holding positions to the rear, were exhorting them loudly, with not infrequent usage of profanity, into wading out into the river as the escaping heretic had done. But for one or another reason none of the Shebite soldiers quite wished to do that—some thought they were getting colds, and others were of the opinion that their steeds could not swim. And while they were all talking it over, Oolb Votz guided his wet, and rather angry, lizard up the farther bank and off into the desert as fast as it could waddle.

Which, while it really wasn't very fast, would seem to be fast enough—considering the rather marked lack of enthusiasm wherewith the Shebite soldiery was prosecuting the pursuit.

It was annoying, how long it took the sun-star Kylix to descend the sky at this particular latitude and time of the year, reflected the Wizard to himself.

They had paused a way into the desert, and dismounted, to give the exhausted lizard a chance to catch its breath again. And they were standing around anxiously examining the terrain behind them. There they could plainly see a plume of dust rising into the clear, cloudless skies. The sort of dust-plume frequently raised by the hooves of a pursuing band of soldiers. It was really not progressing very rapidly, as they saw, but it *was* progressing—and right smack in their direction.

There had been a number of attempts, earlier on, on the part of the Shebite cavalry, to ride off in one or another direction, just so long as it happened to be the *wrong* direction; but the officers had made short work of those tactics. Quite likely, the officers were no more anxious than were the soldiers to catch up to a powerful and potent Wizard, it being an adage frequently quoted here in the south that "A cornered Wizard is a dangerous Wizard." But they were, after all, the ones in charge, and the responsibility for catching the runaways was theirs. And, just possibly, when issuing his orders the High Holy Hierarch had mentioned something about "heads rolling" or "boiling in oil" or some similarly unpleasing form of disciplinary action to be taken in case of failure.

"I give them another twenty minutes," complained the simurgh. "Oolb Votz, isn't that fat reptile of yours ready to go yet? If he doesn't catch his breath soon, we will none of us have any heads to breathe with, before long—"

The Wizard, however, was not listening. Nor was he looking—that is, in the direction of their rear where that approaching plume of dust held the interest of his companions.

He was looking at another plume of dust, and this one was in front of them. It was a rather odd-looking plume of dust, and it was certainly behaving in a most peculiarly unplume-like manner, twisting and coiling in a smallish spiral. Anyone else but a Wizard might have considered it to be a small, harmless, and not very interesting whirlwind. But the Wizard thought it looked like something else.

He dipped into his saddlebags and drew out his fat black greasy little book of spells, and began to leaf through it, absently, mumbling under his breath things like: "*Demons*, Spells Against . . . *Derdekea*, Invocations To . . . *Diamond*, Magical Properties Of . . . *Dibburiel* (See Under *Radueriel*) . . . *Dittany*, Pharmaceutical Values Of . . . *Divining Rod*, How to Use . . . *Dizzy Spells*, Cure For . . . Ah! . .. Here we are, *Djinns*, Varieties Of, and How to Get Along With . . . Hmm . . . Hmmm . . . *Hmmmph!*"

"What," demanded the simurgh, "do you think you are doing—*reading?*—at a time like *this?*"

"If you don't mind," said the Wizard with enormous dignity, "what direction is that?" He pointed toward the little whirlwind.

"South," snapped the simurgh.

"South . . . south," murmured the Wizard abstractedly, leafing rapidly through his fat, greasy black book of spells. "Probably under the Principate of the angel

Darkiel, since he guards the gates of the South Wind . . . well, it's worth a try, anyway—"

And, gathering himself up to his full height (such as it was), the Wizard strode out until he stood directly in the path of the little whirlwind, which was meandering lazily along, threw up his right hand with an impressive gesture, and addressed the whirlwind in a loud, commanding voice—

"*Hail*, O Spirit of the Air!"

"Who," groaned the bird, "do you think you are talking to?"

"To *him*," hissed the Wizard between clenched teeth. "He's a Desert Djinn—one of the Unclean Spirits of the Air, although under the present circumstances, I don't think it would be exactly politic to mention the fact—I address you, O Spirit, in the Name of Darkiel thy Master!—Halt in thine eternal wanderings, and assume thine true and rightful form, I beseech thee!"

Ooo squeaked. The simurgh blinked three times rapidly, thought about hiding his head under his wing, thought better of it. The whirlwind stopped whirling, letting all of its dust fall to the ground, and became a tall, cloudy shape that towered up to a height of about twelve feet. Gradually darkening, thickening, taking on shape and hue and substance, it assumed the likeness of a gigantic human figure, quite spectacularly male and quite spectacularly naked, but with two cloven hooves instead of feet with toes on them, and a remarkably ugly face, all tufts of bright green beard, enormous pointed ears, a bald head from whose temples sprouted two huge curling horns like those of a ram, and round, goggling eyes like balls of crimson fire. *Three* eyes, in fact.

There was also a mouth. Quite a lot of mouth, and a lipless one, that stretched almost from prick-ear to prick-ear. And in the mouth were an awful lot of teeth, bright yellow, and more like the tusks of a boar than human teeth.

"Hail, O Mortal," it replied politely, in a voice so deep that it made the ground shake ever so little. "Why stoppest thou me in mine wanderings—and why hailest thou me in the Name of Mighty Darkiel, the Prince and Potentate of my Kind?"

"Oh, just wanted to say 'hello,'" said the Wizard, amiably. "How's tricks, anyway?"

The Djinn observed in ponderous tones that everything was pretty much okay with the Djinns. The two fell into polite conversation, during which the Djinn squatted tailor-fashion on the ground in front of the Wizard, so that the latter would not have to crane his neck so uncomfortably while looking up and talking with him.

And all the time the soldiers were getting closer.

"I noticed you were kicking up some dust," remarked the Wizard. "Not much dust, though. So I figured you were probably pretty small and puny, for a Djinn. Big, strong Djinns ought to be able to raise an awful lot of dust, I imagine. Too bad you're so weak and feeble, though—"

"Weak and feeble—*I?*" demanded the Djinn, as if it could hardly believe its enormous pointed ears. Three red eyes rolling, it glared down at the fat little man. "Know, O Mortal, that Eforkiel of the Green Beard—that's me, you understand—is among the Greatest and Most Powerful of all the Thousand Djinns which haunt the Desolation of Yu! I have crushed little pipsqueaks like you into the dust for less provocation—"

"Prove it," yawned the Wizard.

"Huh?" The Djinn blinked, mouth gaping incredulously. "You mean you want me to crush you into the dust?" the creature inquired, looking amazed.

"Not at all," said the Wizard. "If you can raise a mighty dust storm, let's see you—right about over there, where all those soldiers are. Put up or shut up, Eforkiel, you big faker! Personally, I don't think you can raise more than a few handfuls of this sand—it looks pretty darn heavy to *me.*"

"I'll show you," blustered the Djinn. And it began to spin around on its toes—the points of its hooves, I mean—dissolving back into empty air again, but whipping up a lot of sand as it did so. It became a mighty pillar of whirling cloud, and granules of sand began to hiss through the air as the wind sucked them up.

The Wizard pulled the cowl of his robe up over his face, and gesturing to his friends to climb back on the lizard, did so himself, thumping his heels in the lizard's fat ribs. It began plodding off into the south.

Behind them, the Desert Djinn—now a tremendous pillar of whirling cloud, darkening to thundery and ominous hues, went marching across the sand toward the soldiers, who all stopped in consternation to see it come.

In no time it had raised a vast cloud of gritty sand that shrieked shrilly through the air, hiding the soldiers from the escaping Wizard and his friends, and hiding the escaping Wizard and his friends from the soldiers. In fact, the entire horizon dimmed and vanished behind a colossal sand storm that rose to the very heavens and blocked away the world like a dim but solid wall that stretched from east to west.

If the soldiers were as smart as they seemed to be, they undoubtedly turned tail and went back to Sheb as fast as they could—riding right over their protesting officers, it might well be. At any rate, neither the Wizard nor his companions ever saw them again.

And the sand storm lasted all night.

"They are unpleasant and malicious creatures, on the whole," the Wizard remarked under the moonlight as they toasted frankfurters over a crackling fire he had conjured up, as he had also, of course, conjured up the frankfurters. "But they are also rather dumb and dim-witted, and easily talked in—or out—of anything. Their sin was the sin of pride, and they can usually be tricked through an appeal to their pride or their vanity, for they possess both in considerable amounts. Eforkiel will enjoy having demonstrated his prowess, and will feel gratified to have proven his strength, when challenged. And it will never occur to him to come looking for me when he is tired of sand storming—in fact, by this time, the poor fellow has probably forgotten all about me, and is wondering what prompted him to make a sand storm in the first place. They also have very poor memories, you see."

"You talk too much," observed the simurgh, chewing

on the end of a frankfurter whose other end he held daintily between his claws.

"I know," said the Wizard comfortably. "But it is one of the least of my faults, and among the more lovable."

"All the world loves a fat man," Ooo said solemnly.

"That's true," grinned the Wizard. "Another frankfurter, my dear?"

"Please."

III.

GAMAR AND THE GOBLINS

7.

Concerning a River named Zong, a Jungle named Glash, a Village called Yan, and a Captive Warrior known as Gamar

They slept that night out under the stars, in hammocks rigged by the Wizard, who warned that this region of desertland was the haunt of small, two-horned, and quite venomous serpents called cerastes.

Since there was nothing to hang the two ends of the hammocks upon, they hung them from nothing. A stern word from Oolb Votz apparently solidified the air to an extent sufficient to support their weight. Snuggling down in the swaying hammock, the Wild Girl reflected yet again, and drowsily, that it is certainly a great convenience to have a Wizard along with you on adventures and quests and things—if you are going to have adventures and quests and things, that is.

She slept soundly, as did they all, except that she would really rather have shared her hammock with Oolb Votz. It had, after all, been a couple of nights now since they had last slept together, and Ooo was a girl of regular habits and of healthy appetites. The Wizard explained, fondly, that two in a hammock is just about one too many; and, anyway, he was a bit too corpulent for such aerial acrobatics.

"And, my dear *chela*, during a tender moment it would certainly break the mood did we, in our enthusiastic abandon, pitch either you or me out onto our heads—or any other portion of our anatomies!"

Ooo shrugged and grinned and was about to suggest they give it a try. Whereupon he gently reminded her about the night-wandering serpents. Thereafter, her enthusiasm for a bout of aerial gymnastics waned rather markedly.

The following day they followed the desert south until they came to the banks of a river. This, the Wizard announced complacently, was the River Zong, to which the Tsa which they had crossed yesterday afternoon with the soldiery of Sheb more or less on their heels, served as a tributary. The complacency in his tones derived from his skills at navigating their journey across the desert and arriving at the spot he had originally intended arriving at without getting lost or going astray. This was a not-unremarkable feat to have performed without a compass, and also without recourse to the stars, since Eforkiel's sand storm had blotted out the nocturnal heavens quite effectively.

"In a way, it's rather a shame the Zaoites lack the compass," he remarked lazily after lunch. "It would be such a convenience to them to possess so useful an instrument. Perhaps I will suggest it to some people I know, if I remember it."

"What's a 'compass'?" inquired Ooo pertly.

"Never mind," yawned the Wizard. "It would be too complicated to bother explaining it."

A grove of tall tubular trees, rather resembling the bamboo, grew along the shores of the River Zong, and these the Wizard felled that afternoon, using an Enchanted Sword he carried in his saddlebags. Neither the Wild Girl nor the simurgh had known that he kept any such weapon around: but then, there were probably a lot of things stored away in those saddlebags they knew nothing of, so it didn't much matter.

Oolb Votz supervised his *chela* in the construction of a large raft that afternoon, from the shade of the remaining trees. She tied the bamboo poles together, using makeshift ropes woven from river reeds pounded flat and supple with a stone from the shore. Ooo was quite handy at this, since her tribe back in the Barbarian Mountains had manufactured ropes in much the same way. By sunset the raft was ready to be launched onto the rushing waters of the Zong.

They piled their gear and saddlebags aboard and

seated themselves in the middle of the raft, with the Wizard at exactly the center of gravity, since he was heavier than the others put together. As for the scarlet lizard, his reins were tied to the rear of the raft, and he was encouraged to swim after them. The Wizard pointed out, when Ooo commiserated with the poor creature and voiced her fears that he might drown, that their steed was, after all, a hydrus, such as ordinarily inhabit the upper banks of the Han, and are customarily of quasi-aquatic habits. Ooo did not understand that term, and his further elaboration which employed the word "amphibian" also failed to find a place in her rudimentary vocabulary, but he said to never mind, all would be well. Then he permitted Ooo to push the raft into the river and let her clamber aboard.

They floated off downstream, moving at quite a decent clip, with Ooo only occasionally having to use a long pole to push them free of the far shore or to fend off floating tree trunks.

The sky blushed with color, paled to rich tangerine, deepened to gold and purple. Fantastic birds flew from tree to tree, attracting the eye of the simurgh, who blinked sleepily from his perch atop the Wizard's head. Dinner that night was a rather catch-as-catch-can affair of jungle fruits. They slept rolled in blankets, the Wizard lying on his back with his hands folded atop his stomach, snoring gently. A minor diabolus was conjured to attend them during the night and to see that they did not run aground on the muddy shore or collide with a bit of river floatage, which might capsize them.

All the next morning they sailed down the River Zong. At times the river was narrow, and the water rushed along through the gorges. At other times the banks widened out, and the rushing of the river slowed to a lazier and more placid pace.

The strip of jungle foliage which grew on either bank became denser, thicker, greener, and gradually hid all views of the desert regions, which had anyway, by this time, become more of a rolling savanna or grassland. By noontime they were sailing along through a jungle country which the Wizard informed them was called

Glash. He pointed out to them some of the more interesting jungle flora, such as the stark-white, and leafless, and extremely deadly upas tree, from whose poisonous properties he protected them with a spell. The venom exuded from the bark of the upas was so exceptionally virulent, he lazily explained, that if a bird flying over it so much as touched the Upas with its shadow in flight, the unfortunate avian dropped from the sky, dead as a stone. And, with a slight shudder, the Wild Girl reflected once again on the usefulness of having wizards along with you on this sort of adventure.

As they penetrated more deeply into the Jungles of Glash, some of the fauna appeared. Ooo was distressed to hear what sounded to her like a baby crying, but the Wizard winked and pointed to where a peculiar four-legged creature squatted on the shore, half hidden behind a bush. It was, he said, an ahuizotl.

"What's that?" Ooo asked.

"An odd creature of rather ghastly appetites," he explained with a yawn. "The ahuizotl has a peculiar passion for human fingernails, eyeballs and teeth, and attracts the unwary huntsman or traveler into its clutches by imitating the cry of a human infant. When the ahuizotl's prey comes within reach of its lair, the beast seizes it with its tail, which is long and flexible and very strong, and has something remarkably like a human hand growing out of the tip of its tail. The ahuizotl's grip is reputedly unbreakable."

Ooo shivered, and closed her ears to the baby cry, which receded into the distance as they rushed downriver.

A bit later they spied yet another jungle beast which the Wizard (who loved explaining things to people) affably identified as the aigamuchas. It looked rather clumsy to the Wild Girl and seemed to be always bumping into things, and as its woolly face was completely obscured by hair she could understand why. She understood even better when her mentor described the predicament peculiar to the lowly aigamuchas, who only has its eyes on the top of its feet and can therefore only see behind it, not in front.

After this, the Wizard took his nap and left Ooo to ogle the jungle creatures by himself.

He did not, however, slumber for very long, for the fat scarlet lizard who swam or sometimes floated along behind their raft was being annoyed by a school of rather large and dangerous-looking—and certainly quite odd-looking—fish. The Wizard yawned, blinked, and took a look behind them.

"Nothing to worry about, my dear *chela*," he said just a bit grumpily. "Those are acipensers, and quite harmless to anything so well-armored as a hydrus."

"What are acipensers?"

He shrugged fat shoulders. "A sort of fish whose scales grow on its body *backwards*, that is, pointing toward its head rather than toward its tail, as is the case with most of the other denizens of the deep. For this reason, perhaps, the acipenser prefers to swim *against* the stream, rather than with the current, probably because otherwise the friction of the water catching in its scales would slow it down. They are relatively harmless, and as we are going rather swiftly, we shall be out of the school of acipensers in no time. Now, *do* let me have my nap, with no more of these interruptions! We have a busy afternoon and evening ahead of us, you know, and I must snatch what rest I can, so as to be at my best."

Ooo did not know to what the Wizard referred, of course, but since he usually seemed to know what he was doing, she resolved to let him do the worrying. She continued to watch the jungle go rushing by and, from time to time, she wished that Oolb Votz were still awake so that she could inquire of him concerning some of the strange and curious beasts she glimpsed amid the flowering foliage.*

* May I remind you here that what I said in my footnote to Chapter 2 still holds true? I refer to the quite legitimate fabulosity (if there *is* such a word, and if there isn't there certainly should be) of all of the flora and fauna mentioned in this veracious history. As much as I would have liked to, since they are singularly imaginative and curious creatures, I *did not* invent the acipensers, or the aigamuchas, nor even the ahuizotl. Nor, for that matter, any of the other animals you will encounter in the remainder of this chapter.

A bit later, two rather large and definitely weird-looking animals caught the eye of Ooo, and she gave utterance to a stifled squeak.

The simurgh, interrupting his doze, opened one sleepy eye and blinked at her questioningly—the bird having a while back decided to snatch some forty or so winks himself.

The Wild Girl pointed a trembling finger at the two huge beasts which were, even now, prowling along the farther shore of the river, keeping up with the moving raft, and staring rather hungrily in their direction.

"The bleps and the calcar," the bird drawled, after a disinterested look at them.

"Are they—dangerous?"

"Quite," the simurgh said succinctly. "But they present no danger to us: look, we are past them already, and well beyond their reach."

A bit later on there sounded another squeak from the savage girl. The simurgh opened an eye and looked at her.

"What now?" inquired the bird, testily. The girl pointed timidly, and the bird twisted its head around. A very large and very dragonish-looking reptile was lapping up water at the river's edge. It was entirely flame colored, and had a head rather like a horse's, except for the fact that it possessed four eyes, instead of two. It stared hungrily at them as they passed, lashing its dragon tail restively. And Ooo found it peculiarly unsettling to be stared at by twice the normal number of optics.

"A soham," yawned the bird in bored tones. And then, in response to the girl's obvious but unvoiced query, he added: "Yes, yes, a very dangerous brute—but not to us. At least, not now. The soham has already eaten, and is no longer hungry."

"How—how do you *know?*"

"Because it is among the curious habits of the soham to drink only after it has fed," the bird grumbled sleepily. And before long it had nodded off, leaving Ooo alone and apprehensive. On the whole, however, she may have been fortunate that no one else on the raft was awake and was able to identify for her the other dangerous and crafty predators she glimpsed, such as the syl, a variety of basilisk with a disconcertingly human face. Or the dreadful ouranabad which flew overhead, batlike wings lazily flapping in the steamy tropical air. This last was a ferocious flying hydra with numerous snaky heads on the ends of its several squirming and snaky necks. She shuddered and hid her eyes until it had gone by and was out of sight.

On the whole, Ooo decided that she did not at *all* care for jungles.

By afternoon they reached a jungle clearing, and the Wizard awoke just in time to direct his *chela* to pole the raft over to the nearer shore, where she secured the craft by looping a few long, ropy jungle vines around one of the bamboo logs and knotting it firmly so that the rushing current could not carry it away and leave them marooned.

"This village," the Wizard wheezed, as he climbed over fallen logs to gain the relative security of the shore, "is known as Yan."

"*What* village?" inquired the simurgh, sharply. For, indeed, no human habitation was in sight: there was, in fact, nothing at all to be seen but a large clearing in the woods, a circular, grassy space entirely surrounded by large trees with thickly leafed low branches.

"Be so good," murmured the Wizard, "as to contain yourself for the nonce, my dear fellow, and all will become clear." He strode forward into the center of the clearing with an important waddle, and took a position facing the thicker of the trees. He seemed to be waiting for something, but his companions were mystified as to what it might be.

"Ooo," said Ooo with a little squeak at the end which I despair of reproducing even phonetically. The simurgh peered intently into the gloom cast by the heavy-laden boughs, and repressed a small start of surprise.

For people were watching them from the branches and, in some cases, from behind the trunks of the trees. Rather peculiar-looking people, in fact. They were tall and burly and manlike, but covered with shaggy, dark-green pelts of rough hair, and had thick, curling beards and long manes of hair, also green, which tended to blend with the foliage. They were barefoot and clasped heavy wooden clubs in huge, gnarled hands. They were, in fact, Wodewoses; but, then, Ooo had never heard of Wodewoses, so the term would have meant nothing to her.

"Be careful," the Wizard advised in a quiet voice. "They are truly rather mild and even timid creatures. But they are children of nature and are unable to control their emotions. If disturbed or alarmed, they can be very dangerous indeed, for they are very strong."

"But what *are* they?" breathed Ooo.

"Wodewoses," the Wizard declared. "The Wild Men of the Woods—not Wild in the sense that the Ningites consider *you* to be Wild, for by that term they denote barbarians. But true savages, and much closer to the animals than we are."

He began to perform Magic, making wheels of colored light form and spin about each other, and globes of sparkling, pastel-colored fire drift about like huge, incandescent soap bubbles. The forest creatures seemed captivated by the light and color and motion, and made grunting or gobbling sounds to each other.

"They do not possess the gift of articulate speech," the Wizard observed in a low voice. "Nor are they of sufficient intellect to build huts or other habitations, but live up in the trees in huge nests of woven twigs and grasses. But you will observe that they know something of the use of tools, for those clubs they are holding are obviously clubs, and are carried about for the purpose of bashing people over the heads, should bashment be deemed necessary."

Seeing that the strangers made no moves toward them, the Wodewoses began to lose their fear of them and to emerge, one by one from the branches and the bushes, to squat on their hairy hunkers at the edge of the clearing, the better to observe the whirling, spinning colored lights the Wizard was producing. Some of them gave shy, childish smiles at the strangers and cast timid glances at them, looking quickly away if they intercepted a look from the newcomers.

"Oh, look! They have a prisoner!" whispered Ooo, nudging one shoulder as if trying to point without using her hands. They looked in the direction she had indicated in this wise, and, sure enough, there was a young man, mostly naked and tied up with vines, his mouth stuffed with a handful of green moss, who lay under a large bush casting beseeching glances at them.

"While I am holding the attention of the Wodewoses, my dear *chela*," puffed Oolb Votz in conspiratorial tones, "see if you can leave the clearing and circle around behind my audience and untie that unfortunate youth. I fear the simple savages are occasionally cannibalistic—a deplorable custom, and very unhygienic, but there you are. Perhaps you can get him down to the raft unseen, one hopes, by the Wodewoses. If you can manage it, be ready to cast off at a moment's notice. The simurgh and I will make a dignified withdrawal when you are ready to depart—give us a whistle or something, so we will know—"

Then he produced a fountain of spouting, multicolored sparks that jetted up and up into the air, exploding into a shower of dazzles that spun about like luminous tops. The Wild Men *oohed* and *ahhed* appreciatively, and would probably have clapped their hands in applause, had they known how. The pyrotechnics were sufficiently spectacular to hold their combined attention while the Wild Girl glided surreptitiously from the clearing and went to the aid of the captive. After what seemed like an interminable interval of time, during which the Wizard did just about everything with fireworks that can possibly be imagined, and was about to run out of ideas, the welcome sound of a low but piercing whistle came to their ears from the direction of the river bank.

Summoning up his last reserves, the Wizard created a whirling constellation of colored balls that dipped and swirled and wove in dizzying spirals, eventually coming together into a sparkling explosion, from whose fireball drifting sparkles floated, settling on the grass like floating snowflakes of Technicolor.

The Wodewoses grinned in delight, showing worn, blunt tusks of dingy yellow between their blubber-lips.

"Whoosh, whoosh!" they said to each other, nodding vehement approval.

While they were busy admiring the floating sparkles, the Wizard began backing out of the clearing as unobtrusively as was likely to be possible to one of his not-inconsiderable girth.

"Slowly, now, my dear bird," he wheezed under his breath. "Backwards, if you please, all the way—careful, now, don't do anything to attract their attention if you can help it. . . . No hurry, no hurry at all, plenty of time . . . let us not alarm my bedazzled audience by any hasty or precipitous retreat. There we are, that's it, just a little farther now . . . ah, yes, that's the way . . . a little farther, now—ah! Thank The God! *Do* push off, my dear *chela!*"

Collapsing in the middle of the raft, the Wizard produced from one sleeve a large bandanna handkerchief, wherewith he wiped his perspiring face, neck, chin, brow and pate, while the Wild Girl poled them out into the middle of the stream, where the current soon caught them. In no time they were rushing along, and the Wodewoses' village was left behind. Seemingly, the Wild Men had not yet discovered the escape of their prisoner, for no hue and cry was sounded, nor did any missiles come hurtling through the steamy air in their direction.

The young man they had rescued crouched on all fours at one end of the raft and seemed trying to wash several accumulated layers of grime and filth from as much of his anatomy as could, with decency, be bathed in mixed company, scooping up handfuls of river water for this purpose. He was young, fairly good-looking with regular and clean-cut features, and wore wound about his loins the remnants of what had once been a linen tunic. Whatever his history and origin, he had obviously come through harrowing trials in recent days or weeks, for his tanned hide was covered with weals, bruises and cuts, and he looked quite emaciated. His hair, which was dark brown and, ordinarily, smooth, was disordered and stuck full of leaves. He had, decided the simurgh, good eyes and a steady jaw.

Ooo thought so, too. She covertly admired his

brawny shoulders, and, in particular, liked his strong, muscular thighs. But when he caught her looking at him, and smiled, she blushed furiously and suddenly became completely absorbed in the business of poling the raft free of drifting snags.

"You have had a narrow escape, young man," said Oolb Votz affably, handing to him the never-empty black jug. "Take aboard a little of this, just to replenish the inner man, so to speak."

The young man took a swig, purpled, swallowed painfully, and coughed as if the lining of his throat had been seared by some fiery potation.

"Good stuff, eh?" the Wizard chuckled, lifting one brow.

" . . . *Smooth,*" the youth admitted in a choked voice, taking a second, more cautious mouthful. This one went down somewhat easier, and the third swallow was virtually painless.

"Now that you are somewhat restored (we shall have a late lunch soon enough, never fear), permit me to do the honors here. I am the Oolb Votz, Magister, an itinerant Wizard-Errant from Magic Mountain country, as you have no doubt already guessed from the color of my robes and, ahem, of my epidermis. This is my slave girl, Ooo, a Wild Girl from the Barbarian Mountains beyond the Plains of Chun, currently acting as my *chela* or apprentice. And yonder exorbitantly colorful bird is none other than a fabulous simurgh. May we inquire into your own antecedents, my dear fellow?"

The youth nodded with dignity. "My name is—Gamar," he said, after a hesitation almost too slight to be called a pause, but which the Wizard nonetheless noticed. "I am a Warrior of Yab, currently in exile as my family were favored by the former monarch, now deceased and his place seized by one Vroop, popularly known as Vroop the Usurper. To insure the firmness of his rather wobbly grip on the throne of Late King Haram (of blessed memory), the Usurper, in cahoots with the local Prophet who heads the Yabite Church, had me and a few others of my party declared anathema, and we were driven into exile and outlawry, under sentence of instant execution if ever we should dare return to Yab."

And, with these bitter words, the youth frowned and rubbed absently at a red burn mark on his naked shoulder. He had been branded in that spot with the mark of outlawry, a three-pronged fleur-de-lis, by which, should he ever be rash and imprudent enough to attempt to reenter the capital city of Yab, he might more easily be recognized.

"Yes," the Wizard murmured absently, "seems to me I had heard something to the effect that they have recently enjoyed a change of dynasty down in Yab. Well, my boy, if your sympathies lie with the former, now discredited, regnum (as obviously they do), then maybe you will be pleased to learn that the Goblins are causing a lot of trouble down in Yab, and bid fair to conquer the capital, which I believe is a city called—"

"*Shang*?" the youth demanded, incredulously. "The Goblins have laid siege to Shang? But that's not possible—when did they ever organize into armies?"

"Ever since Gluth the Unspeakable became the Goblin King," said the Wizard. There ensued a considerable interval of silence during which the warrior sat, staring at the river, scowling ferociously and chewing on his under lip, and the rest of them pretended not to notice. Except for Ooo, who was still admiring his strong thighs, and still, from time to time, blushing furiously.

After a time Gamar became suddenly aware that he was being moody and uncommunicative, and looked up, forcing a smile to his somber features. (Ooo thought it was a most charming smile.)

"I beg your pardon, Sir Wizard," the young warrior said. "I have not yet thanked you for rescuing me from the Wodewoses—"

"Tut-tut," murmured Oolb Votz, "No thanks needed, my dear chap! Always happy to do a favor for a fellow in distress. But, tell me, how did you come to be in their clutches in the first place?"

"Well," said Gamar, stretching out comfortably on his back, "when I left Yab I served for a time in the King's Guard over in the Land of Yuk, but tired of the monotony and decided to go north in search of adventure and to find my fortune. I was striking north along the Zong, hoping to encounter a caravan proceeding through the jungles of Glash, to which I hoped to attach myself as an outrider. But it seems to be the wrong season for caravans, so at length I decided to strike out through Glash on my own. This, however, proved a risky business. First a gigantic river snake, called a boas, I believe, swallowed my pack yale. Then my riding yale bolted when faced by a pride of Mantichores, leaving me alone and on foot and without provisions. Finally, as you know, I was caught by the Wodewoses, who intended to cook and eat me, I gather—if, that is, they cook their food, which I am none too certain they do. They fed me on grubs and bugs and larva, which they were forced to shove into my mouth when I refused to partake of such disgusting fare—"

"And which doubtless explains your emaciated appearance," the Wizard remarked. "Well, and now that you have reminded me, I believe it is time we ate. Since it will have been several days since you have last had the pleasure of wrapping yourself around a civilized meal, my young friend, this will probably be welcome news! My dear, why don't you pole us over to that little grassy island in the middle of the stream, and I will see what I can do to conjure up a hearty picnic lunch."

Gamar said nothing, but his eyes glistened hungrily.

The lunch was superb.

8.

Discusses the History of the Sword Adamanta, Describes the Journey South into Yab, and Contains Some Very Interesting Philosophical Meditations

For the next two or three days the adventurers continued to permit the Zong to carry their raft farther and farther into the south. Gamar alone seemed discomfited by the direction in which they traveled, since he himself had been attempting to go north when seized by the Wodewoses and forced to endure their rough and clumsy hospitality. Since his stay among them would have eventually terminated in a village feast at which he would himself have figured, not only as guest of honor but also as the main course, and since his new-found friends had rescued him from this gustatory fate, he hardly felt it fitting and proper to complain: and neither could he very well ask to be put ashore to continue his journey on his own.

There were still Wodewoses in the jungle, not to mention a lively variety of even less pleasant fauna. Alone, half-naked, unarmed, lacking companions, supplies or provisions, he would soon have found himself back in the same predicament from which the affable Wizard had so kindly rescued him. So he kept silent on the matter, although every hour that went by the rushing waters of the Zong carried him nearer and yet nearer to Yab.

The Wizard had outfitted the naked boy from the contents of his voluminous saddlebags, whose contents, by the way, seemed virtually inexhaustible in their variety. Some rummaging about therein produced a worn but serviceable leathern tunic in Gamar's size, a pair of calf-high boots made of dark green and bescaled wyvern-hide leather, a girdle to go about the waist which was composed of iron discs inscribed with protective runes, pentacles, designs, and symbols in half a dozen forms of writing, and a clean loincloth of white linen adorned with red silk tassels. The young warrior, having bathed himself by immersion in the Zong (with a blushing Wild Girl looking determinedly in just the opposite direction), happily donned his new raiment with frequent and heartfelt verbal expressions of gratitude.

There was even a sword. Or, perhaps, I should here employ a capital: a Sword. For it was the very same enchanted sword which Oolb Votz had, a bit earlier, lent to the his *chela* so that she could fell and trim a sufficiency of bamboo logs wherefrom to construct the raft.

Enchanted swords, I will have you realize, are no less a rare commodity upon the planet Zao than they are upon our own world. And, both there and here, such are frequently very famous weapons, with their own particular names and histories. Hence it was not at all surprising that Gamar recognized, from the old hero tales, the distinctive weapon which at length emerged from those well-supplied saddlebags.

The hilt of this weapon was carved from dragon-fang ivory, and in the pommel there was set a kind of gem known as a carbuncle, which possesses the remarkable property of lighting up in the dark—a property, it must be observed, which can upon occasion be extremely valuable to its possessor, especially if he is engaged in any night work.

But it was the long and pointed blade of this sword that caught the eye of Gamar: for, if anything, the blade of the sword was even more remarkable than its pommel stone.

In short, the blade was a long and jagged-edged and needle-pointed shaft of pure, glittering *diamond*. The blade being some four feet in length, it made quite a lot of diamond. Since the gem itself retails, among the jewelers of Zao, for about three *pazools* per carat, the blade of the enchanted sword represented enough *pazools* to ransom a couple of emperors.

Seeing it flash and glitter in the sun, Gamar blinked incredulously.

"Is this not," he murmured in a dazed tone of voice, "the famous sword Adamanta?"

"It is, indeed," purred Oolb Votz comfortably. "And it pleases an old bookworm like myself to learn that the scatterbrained younger generation still occasionally read the old, outmoded sagas!"

"The same Adamanta that the great magician, Ahoob, fashioned in the bowels of the world by Fire Magic, and tempered by plunging its smoking blade seven and seventy times in the black bile of basilisks?"

"The very same," chuckled Votz. "And may I observe, young man, I admire your prose style?"

"The same magic sword the hero Shar used that time he rescued the King of Ho's daughter from the Gnomes under the Mountains of Xux?"

"There is only," yawned Votz, "one Adamanta."

"And you are giving this legendary treasure—to *me*?" the youth demanded.

Oolb Votz nodded sleepily. "Wizards tend to acquire many such mementoes and curiosities," he said. "As a scholarly and peace-loving gentleman of quiet, bookish habits, I have no particular use for Adamanta, so you may have it, my boy. Besides, I have several other sorcerous weapons at home of no less fabulous reputation."

"Well; thank you," said Gamar, rather inadequately.

"You're quite welcome, I'm sure," the Wizard said affably. "Use it in health."

After one more day the River Zong emptied into a large shallow lake called the Ronga, and its swift, rushing tide petered out in grassy, marshy swamps and, I suppose, swampy marshlands. A tribe of Merrows, or Watermen, inhabited these shallow waters, which was not, at first, self-evident: it was not until two strong, webbed green hands with sharp, horny nails clamped onto one side of the raft, that the presence of the Merrows became known to the travelers.

The raft tilted abruptly, throwing Ooo into Gamar's lap. She immediately wrapped both warm, bare arms around his neck and burrowed her face into the hollow between his neck and shoulder, and clung there, squeaking.

The green, webbed hands were attached to two heavily muscled, greenish arms. These, in turn, were fixed to very broad and burly shoulders, also of a verdant hue. Then a huge, bearded face lifted dripping from the waters, and looked them over interestedly.

The face was broad and flat and slab-cheeked, with a mere nubbin of a nose and a wide mouth with blubbery, faintly purple lips, and tusks which protruded over those lips, like the tusks of a rosmarin. Rosmarinian, too, was the bristly moustache above those lips.*

The face grinned at them, displaying an impressive number of tusks.

Ooo squealed, burrowed yet further into Gamar's embrace, and said, plaintively: "Make it go 'way!"

"I will, girl, if you'll just let go of me," said Gamar. "I can't reach my sword this way—"

"There's no need, anyway," the Wizard asserted calmly. "It is a Merrow, or Waterman. They are powerful but friendly, and not at all dangerous if treated properly." He grinned back at the Waterman, and said something in an animal-like language composed mainly of snorts and slobbery sounds, interspersed with sounds like those of a barking seal. The Merrow-man grinned wider, replied in kind, and made no further inroads on the equilibrium of their craft.

Since the peculiar creature obviously was not going to bite them or turn the raft over, the Wild Girl peered at him timidly. If you could ignore his greenish skin and slick, wet, leathery hide, he looked rather like a large, woofing, shaggy-faced, affectionate dog. His bushy mane and beard were composed of spines or bristles like his moustache, but flatter and more sleek,

* The rosmarin is the Zaoic equivalent of the walrus, or seal, or sea lion, or something like that.

and they were shiny dark green in color: they strongly resembled some kinds of seaweed.

He didn't seem to have any eyebrows—nor much in the way of a forehead, for that matter—and his eyes were very large, set widely apart, and were mostly purplish-brown pupils, with hardly any of the whites showing. He did indeed appear disposed to be friendly: in fact, he seemed delighted to see them, especially so since the Wizard could speak his own language.

Submerging again, the Waterman towed their raft into the middle of the swampy lake, where tufts and hummocks broke the shallow water. Then he barked and slapped the surface of the water with the flats of his hands until he roused the rest of his fellows. They popped their heads up out of the lake in a circle around the raft, which was now moored to one of the hummocks, and grinned in unison.

Some of them were Merrow-men like the one who had first caught sight of them, and some were lady-Merrows. The men tended to be huge in the arms and shoulders, with squat necks and dripping, bushy beards. The females were, on the whole, smaller and slimmer of build, with large fat breasts tipped with prominent purple nipples, and no beards, but very long hair.

With their low brows, and snub-nosed, wide-cheeked faces, they were not especially pretty, and if these freshwater Merrows were what the deep-sea Merrows were like, it was hard to imagine what the sailors of Zao (according to popular tradition, anyway) saw in them—except for those with a fetish for breasts, perhaps.

One and all, they exuded a rank, powerful fishy smell which Ooo didn't think she could ever get used to. The little boy and little girl Merrows—Oolb Votz wondered aloud if it would be proper to think of them as "Merrow-minnows?"—were cute and liked to be cuddled. But they were also cold and slippery to the touch, and smelled as fishy as the grown-ups.

The Queen of the tribe was an imposing and very bosomy lady whose name no one but the Wizard could pronounce. Male and female, the Merrows went stark naked all of the time, but, in token of her superior rank, Queen Whateveritwas wore a necklace and several weed-strung bracelets of brightly colored shells, and a sort of crown or coronet of starfish threaded together on a sharp spine and wound about her brows.

After a bit of loud barking negotiation with the Queen, the Wizard managed to procure a sumptuous dinner for himself and his companions. It consisted of raw fish and freshwater shellfish—raw, of course, but the Merrows didn't seem to mind very much if Oolb Votz built a small bonfire atop one of the grassy hummocks to cook the provender (although they did wrinkle up their noses at the smell of smoke).

All in all, they spent a quiet and rather interesting evening with the friendly Watermen, singing songs and telling jokes and stories (the cheerful Merrows had a roisterous sense of humor and loved to be made to laugh). As well more than a few small feats of magic were performed for the Merrows' amusement. Then they bedded down on the raft, lashing themselves in place with thongs lest they turn over in the their sleep and roll off into the lake.

The next morning the Watermen towed the raft to the south shore, and they said good-bye. Abandoning their raft at that point, the Wizard and his companions proceeded overland through the above-mentioned swampy marshes and (I'm afraid) marshy swamps.

At times, when there was enough dry land to make a path of, they walked, trudging along single file. When they got tired of walking, or whenever the oozy mud and gooey pools replaced the relatively dry path, they rode on the back of the fat scarlet lizard. But this they did in turns. The taking-of-turns was necessitated, of course, by the fact that there were now three humans in their party, and that the lizard's back, although broad, wasn't all that broad.

After walking along for some time, Gamar cleared his throat with a small, apologetic sound, and asked rather diffidently where they were bound.

"I had thought it might be a good idea to drop by

Yab and see how the Goblins are doing with their siege," answered the Wizard.

"Um," remarked Amar.

A brief silence ensued.

After a while, the Wizard cleared *his* throat with a polite little cough, and said: "I'm well aware, my young friend, that you are probably not exactly burning with impatience to revisit Yab, since, when we first had the pleasure of making your acquaintance, you were in the process of high-tailing it away from Yab."

"Yes, you might say that," said Gamar shortly.

The simurgh, who had been riding along perched atop Gamar's broad left shoulder, cocked a bright eye at Oolb Votz.

"Can't leave well enough alone, can you, you fat old rascal?" the bird remarked caustically. "Just manage to squeak out of trouble in one spot, and can't wait to plunge into worse trouble somewhere else!"

The Wizard said nothing, most imperturbably. The bird snorted, stuck his head back under his wing, and pretended to go to sleep.

"What are 'sieges'?" asked Ooo. She was riding on the back of the lizard with her back up against the Wizard, bracing herself with her feet against the saddle-bags. She was riding in this particular position so that she could sneak occasional looks and glances at the boy, who trudged along behind them. She did this without seeming to do it, a matter of quick glances: whenever he caught her eye she was ostensibly examining the roadside vegetation with absorbed and fascinated interest.

The Wizard lazily explained to her what sieges were. He made them sound rather like long, drawn-out slow-motion battles—which, after all, they do tend to resemble.

"Oh," said Ooo. Then she added, "They sound rather dangerous?" Her voice rose in pitch toward the end of the remark, making it resemble a question.

"I suppose they are," the Wizard said, smothering a yawn. "But with a stalwart young warrior in our company, armed, let me remind you, with an enchanted sword of proven merit and considerable renown—to say nothing of a powerful and potent Wizard—you have, my dear *chela*, nothing to fear."

"I hope you're right," said Gamar shortly. He looked rather grimly down at his toes and scuffed his feet in the dust, like a schoolboy reluctantly on his way to a tough arithmetic exam.

That evening, after supper, they curled up in blankets by the side of the road. The Wizard had suggested to Ooo that she share his blanket, it having been several days now since they had last done so, but she declined, looking scandalized.

"Really!" the Wild Girl said, breathlessly, with a swift glance to where Gamar, some little distance away, was settling himself for the night under a tall tree. "He might *see* us—!"

"He might, indeed," said the Wizard, indifferently. "And so what if he does? A lusty, hot-blooded youth—I doubt if he expects our relations are what you might call merely platonic. After all, why do you suppose men purchase slave girls for, in the first place?"

"*Well!*" snapped Ooo, snatching up her own blanket and carrying it a brief distance away, before flinging it defiantly down. Rolling her lissom young form up until she resembled an Egyptian mummy in full bandages, she said, "*Men—!*" in the most scathing tone imaginable, and very ostentatiously went to sleep with her back turned to her master.

The simurgh, who had taken in the scene from his perch in the branches of the tree, cackled derisively.

The Wizard sighed, then shrugged philosophically, and took a short swig from his fat black jug by way of a little nightcap. His sleepy eyes had missed nothing of the frequent glances Ooo had given to the brawny shoulders and muscular thighs of the young swordsman, and he knew enough about the ways of young people to have guessed that his brief, pleasurable idyll with the Wild Girl was at an end. He could, of course, have insisted . . . but that was not his way.

It had been, he reflected to himself wryly, however brief, *quite* pleasurable. . . .

Ah, well! One is only young once: and, as other wise men on many other worlds have observed from time to time, what a pity youth has to be wasted on those too young to appreciate it!

After a while he slept.

They continued to follow the meandering caravan road south, deviating only to one side in order to avoid the borders of the Land of Yuk, which lay in their path. Oolb Votz did not wish to waste any time in Yuk, for he had a feeling (or perhaps foreknowledge) that things were going from bad to worse down in Yab, and his only reason for venturing this far south was to see about Yab. After a time they rejoined the caravan route, having passed Yuk by.

It is not within the province of the author of this history to assume the omniscience available to authors of mere works of invented fiction. Therefore, I cannot tell you what passed through the mind of Oolb Votz, and neither can I describe his plans or motives, or delineate, with any exactitude, precisely how much he knew of future events at any given point in my narrative. The utmost liberty the historian can take in these matters is to deduce, or to make an informed and insightful guess, from facial expressions or tone of voice, as to the mood, thoughts, or feelings of the characters whose actions he has taken it upon himself to depict.

Still and all, Oolb Votz puzzles me—and must, I believe, be puzzling you. If he had the power to foretell, with any genuine certainty or accuracy, the immediate future—why, then, would he permit himself and his friends to be plunged so frequently into hazardous or suspenseful situations, such as captivity in Sheb, pursuit in Ning, and broiling by dragons? Surely, not just that the future narrator of this history should have at his disposal a variety of vivid and exciting events to narrate?

Of course, it is understandable that his foreknowledge of the adventures through which he has passed in this book might also have included the information that he would survive each peril unscathed. Still and all, is it human nature to risk danger, discomfort, dungeoning and possibly being digested by dragons—when you don't have to?

I wonder.

An immortal, it suddenly occurs to me (and Oolb Votz, if perhaps not gifted with absolute immortality, at least enjoys a life span of enviable and interminable prolongation), might find his existence a tedious matter, if conducted with uninterrupted comfort and in conditions of unrelieved safety. An occasional peril or close call, or risky venture, would add a certain spice to what otherwise might be considered an intolerably boring span of centuries. Even mortals such as my reader and myself, who may (unfortunately) only measure their life expectancy in decades rather than millennia, have been known to leave the comfortable tedium of everyday life in the confines of their homes, to venture into journeys, trips and foreign tours.

At such times, they face the known perils the tourist reputedly faces in foreign climes: the local water supplies are generally not to be trusted for fear of Montezuma's Revenge, the tipping situation is not what it is back home, the natives stubbornly persist in refusing to understand the English language, revolutions have a nasty way of breaking out without the slightest advance warning, and where can you find a decent Martini or hamburger and french fries among all those weird restaurants?

Yet tourism flourishes: people persist in quitting the easy chair to attempt the Matterhorn, legs are broken on ski slopes the world over when no one forces you to go *up* the filthy things in the first place, and the North Poles and Matto Grossos of this world do manage to get explored by intrepid citizens who would just as easily stay home and mow the lawn and paint the trellis, instead.

If such hazards are dared or endured by vacationing mortals, what adventures may not be faced with relish and gusto by *im*mortals, whose tedium and boredom threshhold is probably no higher than our own?

(I do hope you notice my tactful way of occupying narrative time with these speculations without in any way interrupting the forward flow of my story?

That is, I cleverly chose to meditate on these philosophical problems at a point in my history when my characters are all sound asleep.)

The land roughened, producing hills. The hills steepened—now that I think of it, I am not entirely certain there is any such word as "steepened," but if there isn't there really should be—the hills steepened, I say, into mountains. The mountains remained merely mountains, although they did tend to become taller a bit farther on. The mountains were called the Ronga Range, by the way: a rather unfortunate name, but there you are! We sober historians simply do not enjoy the liberties of imaginative invention which are accessible to the authors of mere fiction.

There was a pass through the Ronga mountains, of course (there would have to have been, to enable Gamar to have gotten by them the first time), and this pass was naturally taken by our friends.

After a time they came within view of Yab. It was a broad and level and, obviously, very fertile plain, watered by innumerable small rivers and streams and creeks and thins, which were, I suppose, for the most part, too innumerable, or too small—or perhaps both—for them to have been given any names. At least the scholarly texts and documents which serve as my sources for this history do not name any of the pesky things.

There were groves of trees scattered about the landscape, and small farms with neatly plowed fields, and grape arbors and whatnot, and windmills, and small villages and towns and hamlets. In fact, the Kingdom of Yab seemed to be rather well furnished with all of the usual equipment with which prosperous and important kingdoms are, ah, furnished.

In the center of the plain stood the City of Yab itself, although it happened to be called Shang, rather than Yab, as you might have expected it to be called, seeing as how it was the only city in all of Yab even remotely worthy of the name.

Ning and Sheb, the only other cities yet visited by the Wizard and his friends in this narrative, had been walled, respectively, with purple and red stone. Shang, however, was walled with golden marble—at least it was sleek and glistening, and it certainly *looked* like marble. Right now, of course, it looked rather shabby, with all those nicks and scars and cracks and holes in it, due to the siege by the Goblins.

Oh, yes, I had forgotten to mention the Goblins while listing the various ornaments which adorned the landscape spread out before my characters as they stood at the head of the pass through the Ronga Range—I do hope I mean the *head* of the pass, here—isn't that what the highest part of a mountain pass is called?—well, anyway, there were an awful lot of Goblins.

Several thousand of the nasty creatures, it looked like from where Oolb Votz and the others were standing, and they had all of the usual things armies carry along when they intend to "lay siege" to cities. (Getting all of these technical terms right is very important to us historians.)

That is, they had catapults and ballistae and giant slingshots and battering rams and siege towers on big round wooden wheels all covered with leather hides so they couldn't be set on fire with kerosene or whatever (the *towers* were covered, that is, not the wheels). They seemed to be pretty adequately equipped with just about everything you would expect an army busy with the invading of a country to have.

But they didn't have any tents or huts or barracks or anything like that to sleep in when it got cold at night, or rainy, and that made the scene look odd.

The reason for this was, quite simply, the army was comprised for the most part of Goblins, and Goblins live in holes in the ground, being remotely related to the Troglodytes, and not being particularly fond of the light of day. Goblins are quite nasty and quarrelsome people, with any number of perfectly filthy habits which we don't need to go into here, and among their virtues (if they have any virtues) is certainly not numbered cleanliness. So, at night, they just dig a hole in the ground and sleep in it. Disgusting creatures.

Along with all of those Goblins, they had enlisted a few troops of mercenaries. Some of these were

Dwarves, and they had been hired more or less as engineers to dig tunnels under the walls of the city—"sappers" these are called, in military parlance. Dwarves are not at all nasty, being rather thrifty and hard-working and decent people, although grumpy and bad-tempered at times, and not at all fond of strangers. There was also a troop of Pixies, who served as the archery of the siege, Pixies being terrific shots with the bow and arrow, and at least one company of Trolls, taken on to serve as the Heavy Infantry.

Trolls, you see, stand about nine feet tall and have shoulders like boulders and legs and arms like tree trunks, and weigh about five tons apiece. They are covered by a warty, lumpy, rather greenish and hairy hide which is thirteen times tougher than good leather, and they are strong enough to crush flints between their fingertips.

In short, they are perfect for the Heavy Infantry.

There wasn't any cavalry at all in the army, for nothing remotely resembling horses can stand being around Goblins. (Not that there were any horses on Zao, you understand: they used yales, sometimes enfields, and—when they could get them—unicorns, instead.)

For a long time the three humans, the bird and the lizard, stood there looking down into the valley at the siege.

"Seems to be quite far along," remarked Oolb Votz. "Well, let's go."

"Go?" repeated the simurgh. "Go where?"

"Down to visit the Goblins," said Oolb Votz.

"I was afraid that was what you meant," sighed the simurgh, closing his eyes.

9.

How Our Friends were Taken Captive by Gluth the Unspeakable, of the Goblin King and His Repulsive Court, and How the Wizard Volunteered to Assist in the Conquest of Yab

They were, of course, captured almost immediately—but then, they had not made even the slightest attempt to conceal themselves or to elude Goblinish scrutiny, it being the Wizard's intention to permit himself to be seized and taken before the Goblins' monarch as quickly as possible.

We may, I think, presume to guess how the Goblins felt, seeing a trio of humans boldly strolling up to their encampment. They probably experienced much the same emotion a fisherman would feel if a trout laboriously clambered up out of the trout stream and into his frying pan.

At any rate, they had no sooner reached the outermost perimeter of the Goblin camp than they were seen by the sentinels, who raised a shrill clamor and came hopping out to capture them, brandishing various spiky and metallic weapons. To the Goblins they surrendered meekly. The ungainly creatures had, at first, gawked incredulously at the approaching humans, who came sauntering into view as if out for a Sunday stroll, with apparent calmness and no slight sign of fear. They had exchanged wondering glances, each to each, with their huge, goggling eyes, and yammered amazed remarks to each other, then closed in to seize the captives.

The humans surrendered meekly and seemingly without a qualm, as Oolb Votz had sternly instructed them to do. All of them, that is, save for Gamar, who was extremely reluctant to yield up the enchanted sword, Adamanta, to their sticky claws—and also Ooo, who rather understandably shrank shudderingly back from the clammy touch of the Goblins. She did not like to feel their paws upon her body when they bound her hands behind her back.

Through the brief ordeal, however, Oolb Votz cautioned his companions to submit without trouble, and to be of good cheer. Well . . . they submitted, anyway.

Then they were led through the Goblin army, presumably to a place where the leader of the repulsive creatures would question them and thence decide their fate, if any. Neither Ooo nor Gamar had ever chanced to see any Goblins up this close, and they stared rather impolitely at the peculiar little monstrosities with open curiosity and, I fear, undisguised revulsion.

Goblins stand nearly breast-high on a full-grown man, and are of spindly build, with long skinny arms and legs. They are hateful little creatures, with the most revolting habits imaginable, and they are not at all pleasant to look upon. Generally, they go stark naked—which doesn't make them any prettier—and their lean, almost skeletal bodies are covered with a slick, greasy hide colored a grisly dead white, with an ever-so-slight greenish tint like the mold that grows on stale bread.

Not only that, but they have no body hair at all, which somehow makes them look even nakeder (if there *is* such a word), and their heads are bulbous-browed and peculiarly misshapen, their faces narrowing down to pointy little chins. They have mouths that stretch from ear to ear, like lipless, pale gashes, or the wounds made in the bodies of dead men who cannot bleed. These mouths are usually open, and are crowded with altogether too many teeth—fangs, more properly—which are long and thin and straight as so many bone-white needles. A clear, gluey venom leaks continually from these fangs. (The bite of a Goblin drives men mad.)

To make matters even worse, they have enormous flapping prick-pointed ears, like the outstretched wings of albino bats, and perfectly gigantic goggling and lidless eyes, with vertically slit cat-pupils. These horrible eyes, filled with mocking and malicious cruelty and an awful sort of reptilian glee, glare coldly green or red, and glow brightly in the dark (to encounter any of the creatures on a dark night would remind you or me of an ungainly herd of perambulating stop-and-go signs).

They converse by hooting and gobbling and gurgling to each other, and make the most disgusting noises imaginable. They are unclean, vile-tempered, given to explosions of furious rage, cruel, malicious, spiteful, and, quite simply, the nastiest sort of beings you can think of. Oh, I forgot to mention that they possess no sexual organs of any kind—which might help to explain why their tempers are so vile.

They also smell bad.

These particular Goblins were dressed for warfare. That is, while their gaunt, obscene bodies were still naked, they wore heavy leather gloves studded with spikes, and spiked belts, and horned helmets, and peculiar contrivances on their feet which resembled spurs. To their belts were fashioned barbed-wire whips, knobby clubs, and flat, curved throwing weapons very much like boomerangs, whose edges were honed to knife sharpness. They ogled the prisoners as they were marched through the host, and hooted and honked to each other, making obscene gestures.

Not at all the sort of people you would care to be captured by.

And so they were led into the encampment, the Wizard, the Wild Girl and the young swordsman, Gamar. As for the simurgh, the bird was no longer with them, for Oolb Votz had instructed his feathered friend to fly away and conceal himself before they came to the attention of the Goblins. He had feared the spindly-legged imps would kill the bird out of hand; also, just in case his plans were to go awry, it was wise to have an ace up your sleeve, or a bird up a tree, anyway. Passing the cockpots, wherein the remains of captured yales were stewing, the Wizard was glad he had also set free the scarlet lizard, who might otherwise have faced the same grisly fate. By now he had grown quite fond of the waddling, bad-tempered hydrus, and would not at all have been happy to have had his faithful steed end up in the digestive systems of a bunch of Goblins.

They had left the lizard splashing and gurgling happily in a shallow, muddy river at the head of the valley where, it was to be hoped, they would find him again, if ever they got out of the clutches of Goblinry.

The chief of the army and monarch of the Goblins, who was aptly named Gluth the Unspeakable, differed from his subjects in several ways: for one thing, he was considerably taller and longer of arm, and for another he was monstrously fat. He was also remarkably ugly—and, in a race never noted for beauty, to be outstandingly ugly is difficult to accomplish. He managed the trick mostly by being hideously scarred; one raw pink welt went zigzagging through the middle of a ruined left eye, leaving a gangrenous socket. Another snagged the right corner of his mouth, drawing it into a ghastly, mirthless grin, and disclosing dirty-colored and broken fangs. Ooo shuddered and felt sick to her stomach at the very sight of him.

This Gluth the Unspeakable had replaced on the Goblin throne a former monarch who had been known as Quoor the Nauseating—his demise had reputedly been accomplished by means of a subtly administered decoction of cockatrice venom—who had himself displaced one Ung the Horrible, who had murdered Uk the Ugly, who had knifed Poob the Unpopular, who had strangled Kakk the Loathsome. I could go on with the dynastic sequence, but I imagine you have by this point deduced that the royal succession among the Goblins is seldom conducted amicably.

Gluth squatted there on a mound of skulls, fondling a flayed child, and looked them over in silence. It is not altogether a pleasant experience to be looked over by one coldly-glaring, blood-red eye the size of an automobile headlight, and by one pus-filled socket, but our friends made the best of it.

Insofar as his mangled features were capable of rendering the several shades of expression—which was not very far—Gluth looked puzzled. He probably wondered why his enemies should put themselves within his grasp without a flight or a fight, or perhaps both. Gluth was able to understand human speech well enough, and could manage to make himself more or less understood in it, and his first question confirmed the prisoners' guess that he was puzzled.

"Why you-um no fight or run away, like other man-things?" he growled in a thick, phlegmy voice.

"Why should friends flee from friends?" returned the Wizard in an affable tone of voice.

This reply only puzzled Gluth the more, and he scratched his obese and wobbling paunch as if thereby to stimulate the cogitative processes.

"Gluth no friends with no man-things," he pointed out reasonably.

"Perhaps Gluth does not know who his friends are," countered the Wizard.

"Gluth no got no friends, no-how," riposted the Goblin King. A double negative, you will observe: but then, royalty may be excused such minor grammatical lapses.

"I am Gluth's friend," announced the Wizard.

"Who you?" questioned Gluth, cunningly. He had been getting around to this question in his roundabout way for some time.

"The most powerful magician in the world," said Oolb Votz without the slightest qualm or twinge of modesty.

"No you-um not, neither," declared Gluth in positive tones. "Plopp is."

"I am not acquainted with the renowned Plopp," admitted the Wizard. "But whoever he may be, I can best him in a Duel of Magic two falls out of three."

"So *you* say!" gurgled Gluth jeeringly.

"So I say, indeed," the Wizard said suavely.

Gluth turned to an underling, whom he kicked in the belly with one enormous splay-toed foot by way of capturing the fellow's attention. "Get Plopp," he instructed. The Goblin hobbled away, clutching himself tenderly.

They all stood there for a while, waiting for Plopp to make an appearance.

A ghastly hag tottered up, grinning and toothless, long withered dugs flapping against her knees. She leered at Ooo and fingered her hair. Clinging to her back, a grisly caricature of a child reached out and smacked the Wild Girl in the ear. It looked like an imp.

"This-um my chief wife, Glub-Glub," said Gluth.

"A ravishing creature," observed the Wizard, lying in his teeth. Glub-Glub shrieked and tittered and the verminous impling gave the Wizard a half-witted stare and promptly threw up on his mother, who gave him a crack along the head that would have pulverized a bison's skull.

"That-um my son, Dung."

"An aptly named little rascal," smiled the Wizard. After a moment he added: "Kitchy-koo!" The scabby imp began to blubber.

From some distance away, hoarse voices were heard screaming. They certainly sounded human, but the prisoners hoped they were not.

"Din-din," grinned Gluth, cocking a filth-encrusted thumb in the direction from which the cries had come. "We boil-um up!"

"I should certainly hope so," the Wizard observed. "Raw meat is so indigestible."

Exhausting his store of conversational amenities, Gluth peered absently around, scratching his greasy crotch.

"Nice day," remarked the Wizard.

"Um," said Gluth absently.

"Pleasant weather we've been having."

"Umph," said Gluth.

"And how is your siege going?" the Wizard inquired politely.

Gluth displayed grudging animation at this query.

"Go-um pretty good," he grinned. "Kill-um lotsa man-things! Knock-um in head! Kick-um in gut! Stomp-um!"

"Ah? Splendid, splendid," the Wizard nodded amiably. "It was to assist in your glorious triumph over the city of Shang that my accomplices and I ventured into these parts."

"So *you* say," pointed out Gluth, searchingly. Then, reverting to his former topic, he repeated with gusto, "Kill-um lotsa man-things. Kill-um, and eat-um," he added lecherously.

"The Goblinish cuisine," agreed the Wizard appreciatively. "I look forward to enjoying some of your native delicacies. The victory feast, you know. We came here to help you win the war—"

"No need-um no he'p," Gluth said firmly. "Us kill-um and stomp-um. No need-um no magic! Kill-um wiv-out no help magic." He sounded very positive on this point, adding with gloating relish, "Kill-um, and eat-um."

It was obvious that something in the nature of a conversational impasse had been reached. Fortunately, the renowned Plopp arrived on the scene at this point. He was an aged, enfeebled Goblin with a bent spine and a stiff leg which he dragged behind him through the mud. A tastefully arranged necklace of human teeth and finger bones clanked and clattered about his wattled throat. Both eyes were almost gummed shut by rheum and from time to time the shaman coughed glutinously, spittle leaking down his chin.

Atop his head he wore a crown of dirty, mud-bespattered feathers. In one bony claw he clutched a wooden rattle filled with human knuckle bones. This he shook warningly at Oolb Votz, who ignored the gesture with dignity.

"Ah, my colleague Plopp, I presume?" said the Wizard with a disdainful sniff, looking the creature up and down disapprovingly.

"Me Plopp," cackled the old shaman.

"I'm sure you do," remarked the Wizard thoughtfully.

Just then a Troll came trudging up, big as a house, and smelling like a pit of snakes. The creature had long, matted, stringy hair hanging down to what would have been its waist, if it had had a waist, which it didn't. In one enormous fist it clutched a knobbed club two men couldn't have lifted if they had wanted to.

"Chief, sojers, come," the Troll announced, in a voice so low and deep it made the prisoners' teeth ache.

"Whay-at, Blumbo?" inquired Gluth.

The Troll gestured clumsily in the direction of the south wall of Shang in the middle distance. A postern gate could just be seen in this wall. Therefrom a small party of mounted archers could be observed galloping on their nimble yales, with a pack of Dwarves scurrying out from under their flying hooves.

"That, a-way," rumbled the Troll. It turned a green, wart-studded, slab-sided face upon the prisoners in dull-witted curiosity, as if only just becoming cognizant of their presence. The face was the size of a side of beef, with tiny weak pink eyes buried in deep pits of gristle, and a ponderous proboscis of a nose as long as a man's arm, and three times as thick.

"Go get-um," growled Gluth, heaving himself up from the comfy pile of skulls he had been squatting on. He flung away the flayed infant he had been absently fondling and grabbed up a long piece of iron whose shaft terminated in any number of rusty hooks and sharp spikes.

In no time the honor guard of the Goblin monarch had gone trotting off in the direction of the Yabite incursion, at the heels of their waddling war chief, and the prisoners were left alone—except for the mumbling hag, the impling, the old shaman, and the huge, dull-witted Troll, who continued to gape at the humans, his prognathous, Neanderthaloid jaw sagging, blubber-purple lips hanging down to disclose a tottering row of blunt yellow tusks.

"Who, you, folks?" inquired the deep-voiced Troll after a time, with long hesitances between each monosyllable which I will cleverly indicate by a novel employment of commas.

"Alicazam the Miraculous, the world-famous Prestidigitator and Thaumaturgist," announced the Wizard with a grand gesture. "Here to overthrow the untalented imposter, Plopp, with a display of my Wonder-Working Powers, and to lead the glorious host of

Goblinry to a magnificent victory over the stubborn and retarded humans of Shang the Doomed."

The Troll blinked dumbly at this burst of eloquence, lips moving as he painfully tried to follow the meaning of Votz's words.

Plopp screeched, waved his skinny arms over his head, and began to mumble incomprehensible terms under his breath. The Wizard ignored him grandly.

"As Performed before the Crowned Heads of Yurp," he added a moment or so later.

"Yurp?" mumbled the Troll.

"Yurp."

"The Yab soldiers are driving off the Dwarves," announced Ooo excitedly. She had been watching the skirmish with intense interest.

"I'm not at all surprised," sniffed the Wizard. "Those Dwarves are no fighters. No stomach for it at all. A pity, but there you are."

"Now the Goblins are sneaking up behind them by means of a trench," said Gamar tensely. "Trying to cut them off from the city. *Hoy, hey,* watch out, you fellows!" he shouted. "If only I had Adamanta," he said ruefully.

"Those soldiers," the Wizard pointed out calmly, "are sworn to the service of Vroop the Usurper, your adversary and the persecutor of your house."

"I know they are," said Gamar between clenched teeth, "but they are men of Yab, nonetheless—"

"Blood calls to blood, I suppose."

The end of it all came quite soon. Sentinels posted on the walls spotted the attempt by the Goblins to cut off the retreat of the Yabite foray, and lobbed a few ballista stones into the trench. Two or three of the Goblins were squashed like overripe peaches beneath a boot heel, but King Gluth came out of it without a scratch.

The soldiers rode back through the postern gate under a cover of arrows, and the skirmish concluded rather ambiguously. But then, skirmishes generally come to equivocal conclusions, such being the nature of skirmishes. A moral victory, perhaps: or one of morale, at least. And the funny thing about it was that from the way the Yabites cheered, you would have thought they had won, while the Goblins hooted and hopped and waved their skinny arms excitedly about as if their beloved Gluth had carried off the victory. Both sides were the happier for the brief expedition, which at very least afforded them a welcome respite from the excruciating boredom of the siege.

By the time Gluth returned in triumph to where his prisoners awaited him, it was getting a bit too late in the day for a Duel of Magic, and, besides, din-din was ready to be slobbered over. Also, the Goblin King was in such high good humor after his routing of the villainous Yabite foray, that he was in no mood to order the captives impaled or boiled in oil, or drawn and quartered, or even added to the menu as a modest appetizer.

So the Duel was postponed until tomorrow. Neither Oolb Votz nor Plopp the shaman were exactly displeased by this, for both contestants felt a good night's sleep would renew their thaumaturgical prowess and bring them up to dueling trim.

Gluth felt so good about the skirmish that he even invited his prisoners to the feast. Having formed, by this time, a darned good idea of the main course (captured Yabites, that is), the prisoners politely declined.

"Go-um hungry, then," snorted Gluth, uncaringly.

They were confined by the simple process of tying ropes around their necks, and fastening these to stakes set in the muddy ground. There is, after all, no other way to imprison people if you don't have any use for tents or huts.

So, while the Goblins and their mercenaries slobbered and chewed their disgusting meal, the humans dined by means of Magic. True, their hands were tied behind them, but Oolb Votz was, among his other talents, an Escape Artist, and in no time he had them free. They kept the ropes around their necks in place so as not to upset their captors. Then he conjured up a cold picnic of sliced ham, chicken salad with mayonnaise, succotash, pickles, Spanish olives, and several wicker bottles of Chianti—well, you know what I mean.

They dined sumptuously, and slept quite comfortably on the inflatable mattresses he also conjured up for their convenience.

The Wizard himself, however, did not at first seek the embrace of Morpheus. He was awaiting the simurgh, who came surreptitiously fluttering into camp under the cover of darkness. As soon as the fowl came to rest near Oolb Votz, the two conversed for a time in whispers, so as not to arouse either the snoring Trolls on guard, or their young friends.

"I saw everything," grumbled the bird, worriedly. "I was watching from the upper branches of that pausengi tree," he added, nodding his head toward a stately arboreal specimen, which, like all of its kind, grew not in soil but from the bottom of a lake. "That Gluth is one ugly customer," he muttered.

"He is that," the Wizard admitted, unconcernedly. "And what did you think of Mrs. Gluth, and Junior?"

The simurgh only shuddered and grimaced. Then, he asked curiously: "I always thought Goblins were sexless, so how can Gluth even *have* a wife and son?"

"If the repulsive creatures had no means of reproduction, there would, before very long, be no Goblins at all," Votz pointed out reasonably. "Which," he added meditatively, "isn't the worst idea I've ever heard . . . well, anyway, they *do* of course reproduce, but by spores or fission, or budding, or something like that—sounds rather unexciting, but there you are. I think they bud, like certain plants and trees."

"In other words, instead of going into heat—they just, ah, *vegetate?*" inquired the bird, brightly. Oolb Vootz groaned faintly, but did not dignify the remark with a rejoinder. During their previous adventures he had noticed the simurgh's regrettable tendency to create atrocious puns in times of tension or peril.

"Well," the bird grumbled after a time, "I don't know, Votz, you fat old rascal! I certainly hope you have thought this one through, rather than just blundering into the middle of trouble as you usually do. . . ."

"Oh, everything is under control," the Wizard yawned. "Such is my personal opinion, at any rate. And, in case anything *does* go wrong, we always have our faithful and resourceful and courageous simurgh to count on—a plucky fowl to have around in a pinch," he added slyly. Might as well give the bird a taste of his own humor.

Like all who make puns, the simurgh pretended to despise them: at this sally, he uttered a croak of resignation and rolled up his eyes. The Wizard chuckled.

They conversed a bit further, Votz describing his plans for the rescue of Yab and the whelming of the Goblinish invaders. Then, with a hasty exchange of good nights, the bird flapped away to his perch in the pausengi tree and the Wizard rolled himself up in his blanket, found a comfortable position on his inflatable mattress, and went to sleep.

IV.

VROOP AND VICTORY

10.

In Which we Enjoy the Rare Opportunity of Observing a Duel Between Magicians, of the Outcome Thereof, and in Which Gamar Begins to Develop Suspicions

Day dawned, as day generally does, in so spectacular a manner as to seem rather show-offy were it to be encountered among any less significant meteorological phenomena. Our friends breakfasted comfortably on a meal magically conjured into existence: all except Oolb Votz, that is, who announced that he was fasting in preparation for his test of strength against Plopp.

The fast obviously did not extend to the contents of the little black jug, for the Wild Girl caught him imbibing of more than a few surreptitious swigs therefrom. "A little Jutch courage," confided the Wizard, with a conspiratorial wink. Ooo did not catch the reference, being only a barbarian: and even my readers, presumably civilized folks of superior taste one and all, may not have heard of the Jutch Kingdom on Zao, whose fighters are popularly thought only able to fight once they have taken aboard sufficient potables to become fighting mad.

The Goblins, together with most of the civilized amenities, did not bother with breakfasting. Generally, if hungry in the mornings, they might gnaw and slobber over a half-raw haunch of—to give them the benefit of the doubt—yale. But on this particular morning they were too eager to view the duel between their own Grand Shaman Emeritus, Plopp, and the celebrated foreign challenger, whose cognomen they understood to be Alicazam the Miraculous.

It looked, in short, to be quite a show. And the prospect of something a bit novel and spectacular in the form of entertainment delighted the repulsive little vermin.

You must clearly understand that, on the whole and for the most part, the nasty little brutes enjoyed only what might be termed the more rudimentary forms of public entertainment, whose appeal you might call visceral, rather than aesthetic or intellectual. Their idea of a good time, to be blunt about it, was to watch a good gory beheading, or a nice slow flaying-alive, or a jolly smoky auto-de-fé, with lots of yelling and screaming. These fun things, and your occasional hanging or impalement, or burying-alive-in-anthills, or boilings in oil—or whatever—were enjoyed by them very much in the same manner and to the same degree that we more fortunate humans of refined taste regard spectator sports. The lowly Goblins, of course, were simply too far down on the scale of society to have as yet discovered the more cultured and effete pleasures of civilization, like football or hockey. And, while a duel of magicians did not promise to be quite as gratuitously sanguinary as most of their entertainments, it had, at very least, the aspect of novelty which should give the required fillip to their jaded senses.

The Wizard strolled into the makeshift arena cleared for this purpose an hour or so after the throng had gathered, affably chatting with his companions and behaving with a casual nonchalance calculated to unnerve his opponent. As for Plopp, he had already been in the lists for an hour, and was visibly chafing at the delay.

The shaman had been engaged in working out in preparation for the title bout—conjuring up a few whirlwinds, waterspouts and the like. As Oolb Votz came sauntering in, Plopp was busied with an invocation of thunder, but his nerves were so rattled that, at most, he only managed to evoke a feeble mutter from the distant clouds. The Wizard tut-tutted, shaking his head and shrugging with elaborate unconcern, rousing a chuckle from the audience.

The seconds came out onto the field, Gamar representing the Wizard and a Goblin named Lump standing up for the shaman. Both carried towels, sponges and water buckets, and stools for their champions to rest on between the rounds. Gamar also carried the Wizard's little black jug, in case a more powerful restorative than water should be required. The two took up positions at opposite ends of the field.

Before the bell rang for the first round, the two combatants knelt and addressed themselves to The God. I have no way of knowing to which avatar the shaman Plopp addressed his devotions, but it pleased Oolb Votz on this occasion to recommend himself to the The God in His Aspect of Kaphoom the Sly, Patron of Confidence Men, Charlatans, Swindlers, Phonies, Advertising Executives, and All Priests.

Their religious obligations performed, the combatants took their positions facing each other and a line was drawn in the mud between them which neither was permitted to cross. Then Gluth, seated on a heap of cadavers so as to enjoy an uninterrupted view of the fun, gave the nod to his majordomo, who rang the bell which signalled the beginning of Round One.

Since Oolb Votz was the challenger here, the first feat was to be Plopp's, and upon its conclusion it was up to Votz to top it if he could.

Plopp mumbled under his breath and made mystic gestures. Fire blossomed from the wet mud before him, burning from no visible fuel. It was obviously no illusion, for the heat of the ruddy, crackling flames could be felt by the nearer of the spectators. They gobbled approvingly among themselves, and a polite patter of applause went up from the crowd. The effect, if not exactly stunning, was ingeniously contrived.

Votz extinguished the blaze with a miniature rainstorm from a small black cloud which formed itself, in obedience to his will, directly above the bonfire. The applause was a trifle more enthusiastic. He bowed grandly, waving to the throng. Plopp looked distinctly miffed.

He then formed a cloudlet of his own, positioned it neatly above the Wizard's head, and caused it to sprinkle down snowflakes upon the bald green pate of Votz, who conjured up an umbrella and, holding it over his head to keep the snowfall off, next with a wave of his hand conjured into being a small, noisily whistling windstorm which blew the little snowcloud, still sprinkling down flakes, across the line until it hung in midair above the shaman. As soon as it had reached that position, Votz uttered a Word of Power.

The snowflakes turned to hail—hard balls the size of marbles—which rattled off the shaman's bony skull, making him wince.

The applause was quite enthusiastic this time, and some in the throng went so far as to whistle and stomp their feet.

The Wizard took another bow, and Plopp glowered, glared, growled and grumbled.

Exerting himself to the fullest, the shaman created a truly spectacular effect: the mud bulged, lifted, gaped, becoming a diminutive volcano. Smoke belched from its crater, flames spat, glowing lava dribbled down the sides.

The crowd shouted "*fizzfizz*"* loudly, waving their arms . . .

The Wizard squashed it with a micrometeorite, which hit the mud with such impact as to splatter Plopp from head to foot with greasy mud. The crowd went wild, and even Gluth grinned.

The bell rang, announcing the end of Round One. The combatants went to their corners and their seconds scrubbed them with wet towels and fanned them by flapping the towels vigorously in their faces.

The decision of the judges went, unanimously, to Oolb Votz, who took a swig or three from his little black jug by way of celebration. Plopp looked daggers at him.

The next round was considerably more exciting. It would seem that Plopp, deciding that to continue on so decorous a level of thaumaturgy would mean to lose by

* That's Goblinese for "Bravo."

default, determined to take the offensive. With a vengeance!

He formed a ball of sizzling fire and sent it crackling in the Wizard's direction. Taken off guard, Votz merely ducked rather than warding the missile off. It hissed over his head and fizzled out in a mud puddle. The crowd booed him and, for the first time since the commencement of the duel, he lost some of his aplomb.

The Wizard, obviously expecting the shaman's second feat to be basically similar to his first, stood arms akimbo and legs braced, awaiting a second missile or bolt of some kind, determined this time to bat it aside. But nothing happened. Then he began to shiver, and he sneezed loudly. Looking bewildered, he stared down crosseyed as an icicle formed on the tip of his nose. Trying to move, he found both feet frozen to the ground. Hoarfrost glittered on his robes.

Sneakily changing his tactics in a most unexpected way, Plopp had lowered the temperature in the Wizard's immediate vicinity! This variety of thaumaturgical feat is unobtrusive, almost invisible, and again, the Wizard had been taken off guard.

He built a ring of fire around himself to ward off the cold—a pretty feeble and dreadfully obvious riposte, lacking originality, showmanship and, above all, versatility. It was the easiest and simplest thing to do, and the Wizard despised himself for doing it: any wet-nosed freshman at the College of Magical Knowledge back on the slopes of Mount Wu could have thought of something more novel and exciting. But it was either that or freeze solid in the next thirteen seconds, from the rate at which the thermometer had been dropping.

The audience, guessing that Oolb Votz had come off second best, booed and hooted in derision, while applauding themselves hoarse for the shaman. The Wizard looked disgusted: Plopp visibly preened as he strutted about, waving at the crowd.

And now, for the first time, the cry of "Plopp! Plopp!" began to be voiced in the same breath with "Fizzfizz!"

On his third try, however, the shaman came in clearly second. He attacked Votz with needles of varicolored light which stabbed from all directions simultaneously. And the Wizard promptly vanished—to reappear a moment later several yards away, distinctly unsinged.

This won him a round of moderate applause. Plopp looked unhappy: he had hoped, wistfully, to do something to catch his opponent off guard again and rush him into doing something like surrounding himself with a sphere of impenetrable crystal—a trick any bumbling novice would have thought of, instinctively. But the Wizard had extricated himself from his peril in a refreshing manner.

Naytheless, the decision of the judges gave the Second Round to Plopp. And the cries of "Plopp, Plopp! Fizzfizz!" were growing louder.

"If you don't acquit yourself superbly in the next round," Gamar warned him worriedly, while rubbing him down, "we will none of us get out of this with a whole skin."

"Never fear, my boy," said the Wizard, with forced cheerfulness. "Just watch my stuff!"

But Gamar thought he sounded a bit pooped. Gone was the suave and carefree manner he had worn when first entering the arena: now the Wizard looked wilted, even crestfallen.

And it occurred to Gamar that the fat green Wizard was a lot older than he looked or seemed or acted.

The third and last encounter began suddenly. Heartened by his victory in the Second Round, Plopp must have realized that, if he could win the third, however narrowly, he could still carry away the victory on points alone.

He turned himself into a small purple lizard with a trilobate crest, remarkably like a tiny crown.

It was a basilisk.

Now, this was dangerous, yet almost foolproof, because the glance of the basilisk is so deadly that, if the eyes of such a creature meet yours, you are turned to stone on the spot. On the other hand, the transformation can be accomplished so swiftly, that almost any opponent can be taken in—and petrified—by this ploy.

The little lizard looked about, momentarily disoriented by the sudden change in size. In so doing, unfortunately, he turned most of the Trolls and Goblins in the first row of seats into granite statues of remarkable ugliness—but, then, those who attend violent sports have to expect a certain potential danger from their very proximity to the combatants.

When his deadly, glittering little eyes at last found the Wizard, nothing of the dramatic consequence happened—because the Wizard had, very cleverly, turned himself into a kind of headless man called a blemmye, whose eyes are on his back, between his shoulders.

The basilisk gave a hoarse shriek of disappointment and fury, and vanished.

In its place there appeared a gigantic guyascutus, its massive body completely covered by hard, horny plates of chitinous armor, studded with vicious spikes along the dorsal plates. The audience shuddered and drew in its breath, for this was a masterly ploy and was commonly thought of as unbeatable—since the guyascutus fears nothing in the world, and can be harmed by nothing that walks, swims, crawls, slithers or flies.

The Wizard frowned, brow furrowed in concentration—then became *two guyascutuses!*

The first guyascutus groaned, shuddered, rolled up its eyes dismally, and vanished.

Resuming his normal form, the Wizard also waited—as the breathless throng was waiting—for Plopp's final, desperate trick. He was breathing a bit heavily, was the Wizard, and his bald brow was beaded with cold perspiration.

Then Plopp became a fachan, and both Gamar and Ooo covered their faces. For a fachan is an evil, disgusting monstrosity—the bane of every living thing, filled with hatred for anything that moves, utterly fearless and horribly savage. One clawed hand protrudes hideously from its bony chest; one gaunt leg angles from its naked haunch; one eye glares hungrily from its misshapen head. As for its body, which is covered with ruffled, weirdly contorted feathers as sharp as razor blades, the less said the better.

The Wizard vanished, and in his place a small, graceful, slender animal came into existence: white and dainty as an ermine, it looked completely harmless and inoffensive, peering about with a pink, quivering snout, silken whiskers bristling, sweet dark eyes naive and trusting.

The fachan screamed hideously and expired in convulsions, exuding a noxious stench. Its corpse faded from view and was replaced by the corpse of Plopp.

And—incomprehensibly—the Wizard had won. But *how?*

"How?" was exactly the first question which burst from Gamar's astounded lips as the weary Wizard came puffing and blowing over to flop down on his stool and be fanned. A few lengthy guzzlings from his black jug, however, soon revived him.

"Simple, my boy," he wheezed. "I became an ecidemon."

"Oh," was all that Gamar could think of to say.

An ecidemon is a beast so pure that its sight, or even its scent, can cause the most vile and despicable monster to perish on the spot. (Unfortunately, the Goblins were downwind of the Wizard or he might have exterminated the entire army on the spot. As it was, they suffered from excruciating headaches for days.)*

The Wizard was so exhausted that he had to rest up from his ordeal over the next couple of days, during which Ooo fed him on hearty broths and tasty, health-restoring salads of salutary herbs. The Goblins treated their new shaman with gingerly respect, and left his companions strictly alone.

In a way, this was unexpected. You might have thought them to resent the defeat of one of their own Goblinish kind of a foreigner, and a human to boot. Actually, they were so vile and vicious, and treachery came so naturally to them, that there was not a one but rejoiced maliciously in Plopp's thorough defeat and resultant demise.

Especially Gluth the Goblin King. He could not have

* And if you think I invented the ecidemon, you are very much mistaken. This is a true and authentic history, with no room for inventive elaboration. You will find the ecidemon described in Wolfram von Eschenbach's epic poem, *Parzival.*

cared less, for he had always loathed the scrawny shaman. Gluth had maintained a strict neutrality throughout the Duel of Magicians, favoring neither one side nor the other. This sportsmanship represented no unnatural fairness on Gluth's part, I hasten to assure you. A supreme realist, Gluth had realized quite early on that, no matter what the outcome of the duel happened to be, he—Gluth—could not possibly lose a thing. That is, if Plopp had beaten the Wizard, then it proved him the superior sorcerer. And if Oolb Votz managed to win over the shaman, then *he* was the champion.

Either way, the most powerful of the two either already belonged to the Goblin army, or desired to throw in with it. So, as I say, Gluth chose to favor neither side, because no matter who won, he himself had first call upon his magical services in the Siege of Shang.

And the first thing the Wizard did, once he had recovered from his exertions, was to reiterate his desire to help defeat Shang. Gluth was happy to oblige him and granted his request. As a measure of the royal favor now enjoyed by Oolb Votz, the Goblin King even offered to have a nice muddy hole dug in the ground for the Wizard and his companions. These being the same accommodations the Goblins received, Gluth was obviously placing his new shaman and his associates on a plane of equality.

The Wizard suavely and politely declined, explaining that "mere humans" preferred to live above ground rather than beneath it. If a tent could be provided. . .? One was found among the baggage looted from a Yabite caravan a week before, and hastily erected for their uses. The Wizard and the Wild Girl moved in at once, pleased by the prospect of *not* having to spend another night on the muddy ground without shelter and at the mercy of the elements.

The only member of the Wizard's party who retained serious reservations about all of these recent events was the young Yabite swordsman, Gamar.

He had been alarmed that the Wizard intended venturing south into Yab in the first place. Next, he had been amazed and worried at the Wizard's plan to march right into the Goblins' camp and let themselves be captured. And now he was severely disturbed by the fact that the Wizard seemingly intended to help these nasty little monsters overthrow and destroy the city of Shang.

Even though he had fled for his life from Shang when Vroop the Usurper seized the throne from the former dynasty, once a Yabite always a Yabite was evidently his motto. Love of one's homeland can become an emotion paramount over all others. Such, anyway, it seemed to be with Gamar.

It bothered him that Oolb Votz wanted to help the Goblins conquer Shang, because he couldn't figure out the fat man's motives. Since when did humans side with Goblins against their fellow men? Such treachery was despicable; it even seemed to Gamar close to blasphemy, since it bordered upon apostasy. Yet there wasn't much that he could do about it.

Or was there?

Moodily seated on a rock, kicking absently at a hunk of mud, Gamar knit his brows and tried to think of a way out of his dilemma. Like most young men of robust physique and warlike inclination, he was far more accustomed to physical rather than intellectual exertion. But he did the best he could, and came up at length with several alternative courses of action:

1) He could escape from the Goblin camp and try to alert the warriors of Shang to their danger.

This was the first plan he thought of, and (even to him) it looked full of holes. Suppose he were recaptured by Goblin sentinels, trying to escape? Suppose the men of Shang refused to believe him? Even if they did believe him, what could they possibly do against the Wizard's magic?

The main objection to this plan's success he did not even bother articulating to himself. And that was that he was an outlaw from Shang, and under sentence of death. If he were taken by the Yabites, and even supposing he surrendered to them, they might kill him first and wonder what it was he had wanted to tell them later.

On the whole, this idea looked too chancy. He

cudgelled his wits, trying to think of another one.

2) He could assassinate Gluth and throw the Goblin army into turmoil.

Well, that was a tempting notion, but even Gamar didn't see much chance of its working. He had, of course, been searched and quite thoroughly searched when first the Goblins had captured him and the others, and had been disarmed of every weapon with equal thoroughness. Lacking Adamanta—lacking, by The God—even a penknife, how could he hope to tackle a monster like Gluth? The Goblin King was a lot bigger and heavier than most of his scrawny subjects: he could probably break Gamar in two with his bare paws.

And even if Gamar somehow managed to get to Gluth through all his guards, and somehow managed to kill him, that would still leave the Wizard unharmed and, presumably, still prepared to use his powers to the undoing of Shang.

Which led to Idea Number Three—

3) He could murder the Wizard.

Well . . . he could *try*, anyway: but magicians were notoriously hard to kill. And he still had to face the problem he had found in thinking about knocking off Gluth—*i.e.*, that he didn't have any weapons to do the knocking off with.

All things considered, he supposed that the third idea was probably the easiest, the most practical, and the most conclusive way of protecting Shang from the Wizard's magic. But deep down inside, Gamar knew that he couldn't possibly do it. It simply was not in him to murder the man who had rescued him from the Wodewoses: no, a thousand times no, not even to save his beloved Shang. He just couldn't do it.

And, besides . . . he had a vague presentiment that the Wizard was here for some other purpose than the overthrowing of the city of the Yabites. What his real reason for being here might be, Gamar didn't know and couldn't even guess. But he didn't really believe that the Wizard actually intended to help the Goblins.

At least, he hoped not, and fervently.

Of course, he *could* be wrong.

But he better not be. . . .

When Gamar at last got up from his rock and went off to bed, the simurgh breathed a little sigh of relief.

The bird had been hiding behind a bunch of reeds growing from the edges of a puddle near the rocks on which the young swordsman had been seated while wrestling with his problem.

Unlike most, if not all, of the beasts of Zao, the simurgh had once dared to eat of a rare herb called dittany. To eat of dittany gave one the power to read minds. The simurgh had thus followed the thoughts of Gamar and had been privy to his secret plans. And he would have been very upset if the swordsman had decided to kill Oolb Votz, not only because the simurgh was really quite fond of Oolb Votz, but also because he was rather fond of the young swordsman, too, and would have been distressed if the Wizard had been forced to turn the young man into an ouph.

Ouphs are small, flimsy creatures the size of your finger, man-like, mostly transparent, and completely harmless.

Oolb Votz, as it happened, had turned the last person who tried to kill him into an ouph.

It probably wasn't much fun being an ouph, the simurgh thought. Gamar definitely would not have enjoyed it.

He went off to find the Wizard, who had been in council half the night with King Gluth, laying plans for the overthrow of Shang.

"What are you doing ambling around out in the open like this, do you want the Goblins to catch you?" the Wizard demanded, upon being accosted by his feathered friend.

"No fear of that," said the simurgh tartly. "It's pretty hard to sneak up on anybody in the dark, when your eyes glow in the dark."

"What about the boy?"

"He has decided not to try to kill you, or to assassinate Gluth, and is trying to make up his mind about escaping from camp and warning the people of Shang. But he hasn't yet made up his mind to do it. In fact, he hasn't decided to do anything."

"Good," said the Wizard amiably. "I would have hated to have had to turn him into an ouph."

"Me, too. He's a nice enough young fellow. A bit impulsive and reckless, maybe."

"Just so long as he doesn't do anything to meddle into my plans," said the Wizard. "You keep your eye on him and let me know when he decides what to do. It's no fun being an ouph, you know."

"I'm sure it isn't," said the simurgh.

"You're as light as thistledown, when you're an ouph. A puff of wind can blow you into the next country, if you're not careful. And your voice is so feeble that nobody can hear you, even when you shout."

"I believe you," said the simurgh. "I think he's hesitating over sneaking out of here and into Yab mostly because he fears to leave the girl alone and helpless here, in the clutches of the Goblins. He thinks of her a lot, you know. He's taken quite a shine to her."

"That's nice," said the Wizard.

The simurgh cocked an eye at him inquisitively.

"Is that part of your plan, too? To have the boy fall in love with the girl?"

"Never you mind about my plan," said the Wizard.

A bit later, he said: "Boys usually fall in love with girls, you know. Nothing so strange about it—the two of them, thrown together in an adventure like this, nobody else around but a fat green Wizard and a talkative, rather gaudy bird. Besides, both of them are particularly handsome specimens. Wouldn't be at all surprised if they fell in love with each other."

And a little later, he added: "And what makes you think I *have* a plan, anyway?"

"Usually you have a plan," the bird pointed out.

The Wizard said nothing, rather pointedly, to this. Then, nodding good night to the bird, he entered the tent and went to his hammock. He had rigged three hammocks for himself and his friends, so they wouldn't have to sleep on the bare ground. You could get rheumatism doing that, even with inflatable mattresses.

The simurgh flew off to his pausengi tree and tucked his head under his wing and fell asleep.

11.

Concerns Several Various Escapes and Captures, and In Which the Wizard Plots the Destruction of Shang, and Enters the City Presumably for That Purpose

Despite what the Wizard had said to his feathered friend the night before, you did not have to have eaten of dittany to realize that he had a Plan. And, incidentally, even the simurgh could not read the thoughts of Oolb Votz. *Nobody* could. Not even The God, for reasons which will not be understood by my reader until the end of this book.

No, it was perfectly obvious that the Wizard had not come down into Yab by sheer accident or idle whim, but that he was here for a purpose. Ever since leaving Sheb he had obviously been working his way south, heading directly for the beleaguered city of Shang. True, he had paused en route to rescue young Gamar from the Wodewoses, but any gentleman of humanitarian instincts would have done the same. And it hadn't taken him very much out of his way.

Then again, perhaps Gamar had a part to play in the Plan after all. The canny fowl rather suspected that he did. He had known Oolb Votz, off and on, for centuries, and he knew that while the fat magician liked to amuse himself by mucking about in people's lives and destinies, there often seemed to be a hidden reason for most of the important muckings about he did. (Oh, the simurgh could have told you a tale or two, if he'd wanted to: having accompanied old Oolb Votz on more than a few of these adventurous muckings about with people's lives and with the fortunes of nations, he had put two and two together, and had long ago come up with the proverbial four; but, for all his loquaciousness ((or do I mean his 'loquacity'?)), he was one wise old bird and knew when to keep his beak shut.)

And, anyway, was it really all that surprising, I wonder? Wizards, after all, are—or can be—very nearly as long-lived as fabulous one-of-a-kinds like the simurgh. And, no doubt, they tend to get just about as bored with their share of immortality. Wizards have to have *something* to occupy their time with and keep them busy—some sort of sport or craft or hobby, like crocheting doilies or carving coconuts into comical faces, or trying to invent a better mousetrap. This particular Wizard seems to have made the meddling with and mucking-about-in of human history on the planet Zao his own peculiar and private hobby.

While the simurgh was mulling these matters over, Gamar was similarly preoccupied. He *hoped* the Wizard was here to help the Yabites out of their predicament; but, so far, it certainly looked to be the other way around. He seemed to be ingratiating himself with the Goblins' High Command, and for no other purpose that Gamar could see but the destruction of Shang.

All the next morning, for instance, the Wizard was closeted with King Gluth—if you can consider squatting in the mud being "closeted"—and, from the little which Gamar managed to overhear, he seemed to be talking the Goblin King into letting him get into Shang so that he could open the city gates to the Goblins. This was most distressing to the young swordsman, whose natural patriotism seemed unaffected by his outlawry and exile.

He finally got up courage to ask the Wizard point-blank about this, when the fat thaumaturgist came back to their tent at lunchtime.

"Oh, don't be silly, my boy, of course I don't want the Goblins to conquer the Land of Yab," said the Wizard, rather testily. He had just come from a troublesome council with the King, and was in no mood to conciliate young swordsmen.

"Well, you certainly don't act that way," said Gamar dubiously.

"Of course I don't act that way, you young idiot! How long do you suppose the Goblins would let us wander about loose and unguarded this way, if I made it plain that I wanted to defeat their purposes? We'd end up in the cookpot first thing."

"Um," said Gamar.

"And why in the world would I want Shang conquered by these disgusting and repulsive vermin?" continued Votz. "It is a high, advanced and progressive civilization, or at least it was up until just recently, when it kicked out the former dynasty and set up this greedy halfwit, Vroop, on the throne. If left alone, the Yabites will civilize all of the southern countries over the next couple of centuries, and will probably unite them into a major empire which will influence the history of the remainder of this millenium very much for the common good. The last thing anyone would wish to see, is for the Goblins to crush out the Yabite civilization."

"Um," said Gamar, reserving judgment. He quite agreed with the Wizard, but was baffled by the apparent contradiction between his words, which sounded sincere enough, and his behavior, which looked distinctly anti-Yabite.

"Now, for The God's sake, let's stop arguing politics and have our lunch in peace and quiet. I've been hammering away all morning, trying to drive an idea into Gluth's thick skull, and I'm in no mood for more talk."

They lunched in comparative silence.

The idea which the Wizard had been trying to sell to Gluth was simple but daring. He thought he had found a quick, easy way to make Shang fall to the Goblins. As it only afforded any risk or hazard to himself, he figured Gluth would buy the notion without delay. But Goblins are a wary, suspicious breed, and automatically distrust anybody who tries to do them a favor. Since virtually every other creature on the face of Zao loathes Goblinkind, their suspicions were only natural.

"Beware of humans bearing gifts," seemed to be their

motto. And the gift the Wizard offered them was Shang—on a silver platter.

His Plan—quite simply—was this:

He would enter the city of Shang and cast an enchantment over it, a sleep-spell. Then he would open the gates and let the Goblins in. Nothing to it.

However, Gluth, unused to actually *thinking*, remained doubtful and unimpressed.

"How you gettum-in?" the obese monarch croaked dubiously. "They Yab-men no lettum-in. Them at war wiv us-uns."

"Quite so," the Wizard nodded affably. "But I," he pointed out, "am not a Goblin. The Yabites are only at war with you Goblins, not with their other fellow humans."

"Um," remarked Gluth, slowly digesting the fact. Then: "But why lettum-in, war or no war?"

"A good point," said the Wizard. "They will admit me into Shang because I will tell them that I am a powerful magician—which, of course, I am—and that I have come to assist them against you Goblins. Which, of course, I have not. They should be desperate enough by this time to grasp at any straw that comes knocking at their gates."

"Um," mumbled Gluth, gnawing moodily upon a raw human thigh bone. He wasn't really hungry, but tended to fidget while trying to think, and liked to be occupied with something tasty.

"How cum you'm gotta go in?" he asked, cunningly. "Mebbe cast-um sleep-spell fum here."

"Unfortunately," Votz explained, "sleep-spells are not functional except at close range. And the Yabite archers would not let me get close enough to the walls to cast the spell."

"Um," said Gluth, unable to think of any other arguments against the Wizard's plan. He did not, of course, trust Oolb Votz—Goblins are constitutionally unable to trust anyone, even (or especially) other Goblins, and certainly not human beings—but he could see no way in which the Wizard's scheme could possibly go wrong and hurt the Goblin Cause.

The most that could happen, Gluth reasoned foggily,

was that the Yabites would suspect the Wizard of being a Goblin spy, and execute him. That would be too bad for the Wizard, but would not particularly discommode the Goblins.

They had gotten along without him before they met him, and they could get along without him now.

Gluth decided to sleep on it.

Gamar was in no mood for sleeping on it. Despite the reassurances Oolb Votz had given him that noontime, the young Yabite was still not convinced the Wizard meant no harm to Shang.

Wizards are iffy folk, he knew: there are good Wizards and there are bad Wizards, and sometimes the worst of the lot seem to be the most amiable, friendly and soft-spoken. And Gamar had not been quite long enough in the Wizard's company to know him all that well. He *seemed* a kind-hearted, well-disposed old fellow, but how could Gamar be certain that he was what he seemed to be?

And could he gamble away the safety of Shang, and the lives of all the Shangmen, on the chance that Votz was sincere?

Gamar finally decided that he simply could not.

But neither could he be so ungrateful as to attempt to kill Oolb Votz. The green magician had, after all, saved him from the Wodewoses. He had saved his life, and it would be an act of the deepest ingratitude to take his life in return.

The only thing Gamar could think of to do that might help was to somehow get into Shang ahead of the Wizard and warn the citizens to be wary of fat green magicians.

Of course, they might thereupon lynch poor Oolb Votz on the spot, but that would be *their* responsibility, not Gamar's. His sense of gratitude could only be stretched so far: and many thousands of lives hung in the balance.

So Gamar laid low, biding his time until dark.

As for Ooo, the Wild Girl didn't know exactly what to think. She was well aware of the depth and intensity of Gamar's doubts about the Wizard. For he sat around, glaring at nothing with a furrowed brow, chewing on a hangnail and muttering under his breath. And he paid not the slightest attention to her, even when she slipped her robe down to her waist and gave the upper portion of her anatomy a sponge bath.

If the sight of an exposed, and firm, and extraordinarily well-rounded female breast failed to interrupt Gamar's moodiness, then he *must* be deeply disturbed.

The girl put her robe back on and left the tent in a huff, wandering down by the river to have a talk with the simurgh.

The Wild Girl was lonely, and had nothing in particular to do, and felt depressed in general. At such times, talking to the simurgh seemed to help a little. There was, after all, nobody *else* to talk to—and a simurgh is considerably better than nothing.

The Wizard was too busy with his important plans and schemes and whatnot to do more than give her an absent-minded pat on the fanny in passing. And Gamar seemed sunk in a black mood of glum meditation, or something. So she poured out her young heart to the friendly old bird.

She had been really quite happy with the Wizard. He made her laugh, with his pompous ways and his big words and long speeches—little of which she understood, of course, but it was kind of nice just to listen to them. And with the Wizard around, well, you just never knew what was going to happen next! One minute he was conjuring up rainstorms, or holding conversations with Djinns, and the next he was sailing downriver on impromptu rafts through weird jungles, meeting all sorts of curious and odd and interesting and, yes, sometimes scary people—Troglodytes and Wodewoses and Merrows, and such-like.

Being with the Wizard was more fun and variety and excitement than a circus. But then along came Gamar, and everything changed and an awful lot of the fun went out of their adventurings. . . .

For one thing, just being close to Gamar gave her the goose-bumps, and when he looked at her she could feel herself going all hot and then cold, pale and then fiery red. And her stomach (or perhaps it was some even more sensitive organ?) went all fluttery, down deep inside. . . .

The simurgh listened, and grinned with a twinkle in his wise old eye, and made little sympathetic grunts. He knew the girl's condition well, being learned in the ways of humans. Little Ooo was in love, but hadn't quite discovered it yet, herself.

The simurgh understood love, although of course he had not ever and could never experience the emotion, being the only one of his kind ever created. Hearing her talk about Gamar in her breathless, half-resentful, half-wistful way made the old bird feel a bit sad, and strangely lonely.

After a while, feeling oddly comforted—not that the bird had *said* much of anything, you understand, but it *was* nice to talk to somebody and get things off your chest—the Wild Girl wandered back to the tent.

When she got back, Gamar was no longer around.

And neither, by the way, was his enchanted sword, Adamanta—although nobody noticed it was missing until morning.

That same evening, some hours after Gamar had decamped for the city of the Yabites, the Wizard also left the Goblin camp.

He had finally received the green light from Gluth, and wasted no time in putting his scheme into action, lest the obese monarch should change what, for the lack of a more precise term, we shall call his mind.

Gamar had fled from the encampment at the sinking of the sun-star. Oolb Votz, however, waited until it was pitch dark before attempting the entry of Shang. Being a Wizard, he had foreknowledge of the fact that it was going to be a moonless and particularly dark and overcast night.

He kissed Ooo goodbye, shook hands soberly with the simurgh, paid his final respects to the royal family of Goblindom, and went strolling off toward the walls of Shang.

They rose frowning athwart the gloom, those high

and crenellated walls. Here and there atop them, torches in cressets of wrought-orichalc flared smokily against the dark. Sentinels paced the circuit of the walls and archers sat dozing or playing dice upon the battlements.

It was a mild and pleasant night, thought Oolb Votz, as he ambled across the plain and up to the gates. He was aware of a slight and pleasurable excitement. It was enjoyable to be going up and down in the world, and to and fro about it. For far too long he had remained holed up in his castle, aloof from the affairs of men, busy with his books and experiments and thaumaturgical projects. He should come down from Magic Mountain more often, thought Oolb to himself, He should Get Involved more frequently.

Wizards are intellectuals—artists, in a certain very real sense. Given to contemplative habits, even scholarly ones. Seldom, if ever, do the truly great and powerful magicians mix with ordinary people and mingle with their doings. Magicians are not great travelers, and are certainly not men of action. This was a pity, thought the Wizard complacently, to himself. It is certainly a treat to be in danger once in a while—it lends rare spice to the insipidity of everyday life, and one lives with zest and gusto.

About the same time that the Wizard was sauntering down to the gates of Shang, thinking these thoughts lazily to himself, Gamar was behind those same gates, thinking very different thoughts.

And trying to talk his way out of a hangman's noose.

They had caught him sneaking in by a little-known, seldom-used postern gate. They promptly disarmed him, paid utterly no attention to his loud protests and warnings of impending doom, betrayal, treason and enchantment, and hauled him before the magistrate.

This worthy, a personage named Kang, did not exactly relish being called out of bed at this hour to pass judgment on an outlaw. He would probably have decided, rather quickly, on something involving boiling oil, but Gamar's obvious distress and the earnestness of his words tended to persuade Kang that something might very well be up.

"Oh, very well, then." Kang snapped. "Captain Jork, alert the guard-watch on the walls. A fat, bald, green man in the red robes of a magician. If he enters the city, or tries to, he is to be arrested instantly."

"Very good, yer honor," growled the officer. "And what does we do with this 'un, here?"

Kang meditated, fingering a wart.

"Better take him along to identify the culprit," he decided. "But keep him in chains, mind! The varlet is under sentence of death if ever he dare show his face in Shang again—which he has done."

Jork escorted a grim, worried Gamar from the judge's chambers. They made their way swiftly through the gloomy streets to the command post of the company whose responsibility it was to man the walls and gates of the city. But Jork—to his credit—was not happy about this.

"Seems like a real bummer," he grumbled in a hoarse aside to his captive. "Figger as how yez'd never of come back t' Shang, 'ceptin' t' warn us of this-here magician-feller, right?"

"Right," said Gamar briefly.

Jork's heavy face looked glum. "Got me duty t' do, y'know," he muttered. "If'n t'were up t' *me*. . . ."

Gamar smiled slightly, and shook his head. They rode on in silence to the walls.

Gamar, too, had had his duty to do—his duty to his homeland and to his people. He had been forced to betray a friend who had saved his life. And he didn't enjoy it any more than the guard officer enjoyed his duty.

The Wizard made it through the walls without any particular difficulty, by the same simple expedient he had earlier employed in making his escape from the Purple City of Ning.

There, he had commanded a sector of the city wall to vanish while he passed through. The feat had been somewhat too spectacular to employ here, where alert sentries were certain to raise the alarm if thirty cubits of solid stone evaporated without warning.

So he quietly made a small doorway in the wall, slipped unobtrusively through, sealing the wall behind him again.

Oolb Votz found himself at one end of a black, narrow alley between two huge warehouses. Garbage moldered in fetid heaps; greasy mud trickled sluggishly between slimy cobbles; a scrawny, catlike scavenger yowled and fled, spooked by his sudden appearance.

Holding up the bottoms of his robe, the Wizard gingerly went down the alley toward a small square. In the center of the square a dilapidated fountain gurgled. Windowless walls and barred doorways stared blindly on the square. In one doorway a tramp, reeking of cheap wine, snored phlegmily.

The Wizard paused, looking around himself thoughtfully. He had not been in Shang for several generations, at least, and found himself somewhat disoriented. He had approached Shang from the western side, so this ought to be a division of the city which was called the Jong Quarter, for the good and simple reason that Jongite merchants, artisans and visitors customarily stayed here.

Jong was a small and not very interesting country to the east, facing upon the Deathly Desert and the Cinnabar Mountains, which was known for its black-glaze pottery, jadeite bead jewelry, spices and herbs and perfumes.

However, the lettering on the residences and above the doors of the warehouses was not in the charactery employed by the literates of Jong, but in the hooked and jagged scrawling lines used in a southern country called Zhu.

They carved ivory and mined turquoise and enameled miniatures and trained a variety of small, quasi-human, hairy creatures called aegipans to dance, down in Zhu.

So either he had gotten his directions mixed up, what with there being no moon and all, and had gotten into the Zhuite Quarter instead of the Jongite, or in the generations since his last visit to Shang they had changed things around.

He paused, confusedly, to figure out where he was going and where he was.

Shang was laid out like a wheel, with seven suburbs inaccurately called quarters arranged about the outer rim, and the Shangites themselves living on the inside of the wheel. The Royal Palace was the hub of the wheel, and the Shangite zone—palaces, temples, mansions, tenements, the hippodrome, theaters, wineshops and such-like arranged in a circle about the hub, forming a sort of Yabite buffer zone between the royal residence and the sections of the city given over to foreigners.

So, in order to get an audience with the King, theoretically, he should just walk straight toward the center of the city. He began to do so.

For a city under siege by a gang of Goblins, it certainly seemed to the Wizard that Shang slept rather soundly. True, the town was rather stoutly fortified, and, since Shang was built at the crossroads of several important caravan routes and the warehouses of its large merchant population were probably bulgingly filled with edibles and foodstuffs, nobody was going hungry as yet. But being besieged by Goblins is, to say the least, nervous-making, and Oolb Votz would have expected a few more signs of desperation and hysteria.

As far as he could observe, however, Shang seemed to be taking the current political situation with exemplary calm. Well, they were a sophisticated people, and a devout. Besides, they maintained a pretty decent army.

He got as far as the farther entrance of the square before thirty armed guards jumped out of the shadows and pounced on him.

They used lariats quite skillfully in Shang, he discovered. These settled about his corpulent torso and quite swiftly immobilized his hands. Obviously, if you are going to try the capturing of a magician—a risky business at best it is of first importance to make certain that he cannot make any magical passes or mystical gestures with his hands.

They didn't hurt him, but they trussed him quite securely.

Oolb Votz suffered these indignities with unruffled urbanity. What the soldiery of Shang apparently did not know was that he could work his magic without the use of his hands, if he had to, by the enunciation of certain Words and Names of Power.

He did not, however, bother to do so. In the first place, he was in no immediate danger, for if the soldiers had wanted to kill him they would have bloodied their swords ere this. And in the second place, he wished to be brought before the authorities as soon as possible, and getting arrested was a fairly efficient way of doing so.

Besides, being escorted by armed guards to where he wanted to go was a whole lot easier than trying to find his way there in the dark.

"Izzat the guy?" inquired Captain Jork of Gamar, who stood manacled beside him.

"That is the man," said Gamar grimly, feeling awful and very, very guilty about all this.

As they led Oolb Votz from the square, they took him past where the Captain and Gamar were standing.

Oolb saw and recognized the young swordsman in the shadows.

"*Et tu, Brute?*" he remarked pleasantly to Gamar and they led him by the youth he had rescued from the Wodewoses. Or the Yabite equivalent of what Julius Caesar said to the friend who had betrayed him.

12.

In Which Wars—and Thrones—Are Lost and Won, Hidden Identities Are at Last Revealed, and Gamar Guesses the Wizard's Own Secret but Says Nothing

Once the green magician had been taken prisoner, they marched him into the center of the city and woke up Kang again, so that the judge could decide what was to be done with him. This did not make Kang happy: in the first place, he was getting tired of being woken up; and in the second, a cautious man might just consider it a wee bit risky to go around condemning magicians to death. And Kang was a cautious man.

He decided that the Wizard should be turned over to the city's resident Prophet for judgment. This was the strictly logical thing to do, since the Wizard's crimes, or potential crimes, were of a thaumaturgical nature, rather than civil misdemeanors, and thus fell under the province of the Established Church. Also, it got Kang off the hook.

Now, the Prophet was not particularly pleased to be aroused from his bed in the middle of the night, any more than Kang had been. This was not because he was sleeping, but because he had bedded down in cozy fashion with twin sixteen-year-old concubines, and from this happy occupation he had been roused just as he was —ah—geting aroused, if you take my meaning.

So when he came puffing and snorting out of his chambers into the Inquisitional Hall, an old bathrobe hastily tossed about his bony form, well-worn carpet slippers slapping against the cold tiles, well, you didn't have to be all that perceptive to see that he was not in the best of moods.

"Who's on duty tonight?" he snarled at Captain Jork, who looked blank. "I refer to the Office of Public Executioner, you fool! I am in no mood for long, drawn-out cases. Best to tidy these things up quickly—"

"Ah, lemme see—b'lieve it's Wing Fat, Yer Prophecy," said the captain.

"Good," sniffed the Prophet approvingly. "A handy man with the axe, as I recall! Well, step aside, you idiot, and let me get past you."

This Prophet, by the way, was a fellow named Glibb. He was tall and skinny, with a long white beard down to *here*, and at the moment he looked like someone who smelled something very disagreeable. From the odor of fermented spirits which hung about him like an invisible cloud, and the wreath of flowers around his brows, worn slightly askew, and which he had forgotten to remove, to say nothing of the lipstick on his whiskers, you could form a fairly accurate idea of what he had been doing, or had been about to do, when hauled out of bed to interview the Wizard.

He climbed up into the hierarchical throne, grumbling under his breath, and sat back, glaring.

"What's all this, now?" he demanded.

Jork explained what all this was. Then they brought Gamar out to identify the Wizard all over again. The Prophet Glibb peered nearsightedly at Gamar, who hung his head as if abashed and stayed in the shadows as much as he could.

"Treason, eh? Betraying the city to the Goblins, is it? Dang it all, captain, that's a civil offense, not a sacerdotal one! Dragging a body out of his bed at this *un*holy hour—"

"'Scuse me, Yer Prophecy, but he's one o' them wizard-fellers," explained Jork. "Gonna enchant us in our beds an' let they Goblins in, sez this-here young feller."

"Wizard, is he? Grmmph: that *does* make it a matter for the Sacerdotal Court. Well, you there with all the ropes on, what d'you have to say for yourself, before I pass judgment?"

"I am completely innocent of the charges, sir—which

are, in any event, not only irrelevant but actually impossible," said Oolb Votz suavely.

"How's that? Come again?" demanded the Prophet Glibb, blinking.

"One cannot commit treason," explained the Wizard, "against a realm to which one is neither subject nor citizen."

The Prophet Glibb tugged on his beard, noticed the lipstick on his fingers, tried to wipe it off against his bathrobe, gave up, and uttered a contemptuous snort.

"I'd call enchanting the city and letting in the Goblins an act of treason any day of the week," he snapped.

"But I have not enchanted the city nor have I let the Goblins in," the Wizard pointed out reasonably, "and it is pure supposition on your part, and on the part of these gentlemen, that I had any intention of doing so. To quote the ever-popular philosopher Anon, 'If wishes were yales, then beggars would ride.' In other words, you cannot convict me for a crime which was not committed."

"But the sage Ibid refutes your Anon thusly," said the Prophet with a nasty leer, " 'The rodent in the trap was obviously after the cheese.' "

"Perhaps," said the Wizard, "but the immortal Etc put it neatly, when he said, 'No one was ever arrested for just thinking.' "

"That may be," chuckled the Prophet, "but an empty barrel holds no wine!"

"A fool and his *pazools* are soon parted."

"Maybe so, but three removes is as bad as a fire!"

"That may be, but the used key is always bright—"

"Experience keeps a hard school, but the fool will learn in no other—"

"Vessels large may venture more, but little boats keep close to shore—"

"A stitch in time saves whatever-it-is—" said the Prophet, by now quite thoroughly flustered.

"True enough, but as the Sacerdotal Scriptures put it, 'The moth may flutter as close to the flame as it pleases, but the wick is securely fastened to the end of the candle, and wanders not—' "

"You dare quote the Sacred Writings in my teeth, do

you, you fat warlock?" hissed the Prophet, turning purple. "Take him away—"

"T-to whom?" stammered Captain Jork, so taken by surprise that for once his utterance was strictly grammatical.

The Prophet glared at him.

"Wing Fool, you fat!"

There ensued a lengthy, uncomfortable silence. The Prophet Glibb squeezed his eyes shut, sucked in a long breath, opened his eyes and said, firmly:

"I mean, Wing Fat, you fool."

"Yessir, Yer Prophecy," said Jork, saluting.

They led the Wizard out, chuckling. The Wizard, I mean, not the guardsmen.

All of this noise, fuss and bother had disturbed the slumbers of the majestic Vroop, King of All Yab, whose suites were just down the hall from the offices of the Prophet. The King came yawning out just as they were leading Oolb Votz off to the executioner, and he looked them over with a sleepy eye.

The guards promptly fell on their faces and lay there, trying not to breathe, which might single them out for their monarch's attention.

Vroop was a very fat man with a very red face and a very bad temper. When someone did something that annoyed him, he would as often as not invent a suitable punishment for the crime of Annoyance to Royalty. It was usually something slow and lingering, with a lot of boiling oil in it. The guards used to bribe their officers so as not to get assigned to palace duty.

"How's a body to get any sleep around here, with people runnin' up and down the halls at all hours, and yellin'?" the King inquired of the Wizard, who was the only one who had not fallen upon his face.

"You will sleep a lot easier, Your Majesty," said the Wizard, "once I have disposed of that army of Goblins at your gates with my magic powers."

Vroop did a double take. "You must be one of them magician-fellers," he said perceptively. The Wizard nodded.

"I am indeed, Sire: Glumphwortle the Grandiloquent is the name and thaumaturgy's the game. As Performed

Before the Crowned Heads of Yurp. I was just discussing my plan to enchant all of the Goblins with your Prophet in there. And these gentlemen were escorting me to the dining hall, where His Prophecy was thoughtful enough to suggest a late-night snack might be welcome—"

Oolb Votz grinned and patted his tummy. The King licked his lips.

"Good idee, that," he said. "Wouldn't mind a bit of a snack, meself. C'mon in here with me, Glumphwortle."

"B-but—" said Jork, still face-down on the floor.

"You boys hike down and order us up some grub," suggested the King. "Col' squab on toast, roast boar haunch, applesauce and a couple bottles of champagne."

"But, Sire—"

"Skeedaddle, now! C'mon, Glumphwortle."

The guards got up and skeedaddled: it was not for the likes of them to get the King mad by informing him that he was wrong, and had been gullible enough to be taken in by a smooth-talking sorcerer on his way to a date with the headsman's axe.

Nor, come to think of it, did they care to risk getting the Prophet Glibb out of bed again at this hour.

Later on that same night, at the prearranged hour, the Goblins were massed together before the gates, but far enough away so as not to be spotted by the guards stationed atop the walls.

Not that there *were* any guards stationed atop the walls. Or if there were, they were all lying down fast asleep, because not one shining helmet could be glimpsed from where the Goblins were.

Gluth, wearing odds and ends of rusty armor, with a necklace of baby skulls tastefully arranged about his brows like a victor's wreath, grunted with satisfaction when he noticed the guards were gone. Looked to him as if his new Grand Shaman was about to deliver the goods, after all!

Ooo sniffed miserably: she just couldn't believe that the Wizard could do anything so despicable. And him so nice and cuddly and all, too; and using all those big words. But it certainly looked like he was living up to his bargain with Gluth.

As for the simurgh, he kept his opinions to himself.

The gates of the city creaked open, slowly and laboriously. The orange flicker of a torch appeared in the gloom. By its wavering, citrine light they perceived a fat bald green Wizard in red robes, gnawing on a last slice of boar haunch. He waved the piece of meat at Gluth and made a beckoning motion.

The Goblins began to move. Since there did not seem to be any prospect of a battle, the leaders and commanders of the army—for once—crowded in first, eager to grab the choicest loot, slaves and miscellaneous plunder.

Gluth, naturally, was in the fore. The Field Marshals, Emirs, Beys, Nabobs, Generalissimos, Colonels, Majors, Warchiefs and so on and so forth got inside the gates. All of them, right down to the lowliest Nabob.

Then the gates closed—and a lot quicker than they had opened.

The noncommissioned Goblins, and their mercenaries—Dwarves and Trolls and Pixies—were left outside. They were used to being left out when the spoils were divided, so they didn't think anything of it.

At first.

As soon as the officers of the Goblin army were inside the city, and the gates swung shut behind them, the Wizard cast his enchanted sleep-spell, just as he had promised he would.

But on the Goblins, not the men of Shang.

"Well, I'll be an aegipan's Uncle!" swore Gamar to himself, in a strangled voice.

"Indeed, my boy? Well, you probably know your family better than I do," chuckled the Wizard, in rare good humor. For once, everything had gone exactly according to his Plan.

"So you really *didn't* mean to betray Shang to the enemy, after all," said Gamar. "Sir Wizard, I believe that I owe you several kinds of an apology—"

"Tut-tut, my boy, no offense meant and none taken, I assure you. Ah, look, that's dear little Ooo among the slumberers . . ." exclaimed the Wizard.

And, indeed, it was Ooo. Just on the off-chance that the Wizard meant to betray him somehow, Gluth had brought her along to bargain his way out of a trap with, if there was any trap, which of course there was. The Wizard hastened to arouse her from her enchanted sleep, and she squealed with excitement when she saw what he had done, and ran over to give him a big kiss, yes, and there was an even bigger one for Gamar.

They eventually broke apart, blushing furiously. The Wizard sighed. He was of the opinion that he had just lost a most delectable *chela*.

Then the simurgh came fluttering down.

"Oolb Votz, you sly rascal, I should have known you planned something like this," remarked the bird with reluctant admiration. "The Goblins are getting very worried outside, for it is just now beginning to percolate through their thick skulls that all is not right, something has gone awry, and so forth."

"That's right," exclaimed Gamar, with a frown. "Sir Wizard, there is still an army out there—how have you solved anything by capturing their leaders?"

"An army without its leaders," observed Oolb Votz comfortably, "is like a snake without its head. It may wriggle and squirm for a while, but it doesn't know what to do and hasn't got the brains to do anything, anyway. This is especially true of Goblins."

"Here comes the judge," remarked Gamar.

"It was indeed the civil magistrate, Kang, followed by the Prophet Glibb, and a scurry of chamberlains, bishops, army officers, burgesses, guild leaders, nobility, courtiers and so on. Wobbling along in the rear came fat King Vroop in a yellow palanquin carried on the backs of thirty slaves.

"Good work, Glumphwortle, begad!" the monarch chortled, waving a pastry.

"Thank you, Your Majesty," said the Wizard with vast aplomb, calling the attention of the court to the snoozing Goblins with a splendid gesture.

Vroop the Usurper looked them over interestedly.

"Ugly beggars," he observed. "Give you any trouble did they, Glumphwortle?"

"Nothing that I was not able to handle, Sire," said the Wizard modestly.

"Splendid, splendid! Well, now, we must put our heads together and think of a suitable reward for your services—anythin' up to the half of me kingdom, say."

"That is very generous of Your Majesty," purred Oolb Votz—enjoying himself vastly, as he always did when he was in the center of an admiring throng—"but I fear I shall have to ask for a bit more than that: *all* of your kingdom, to be precise!"

The courtiers gasped, as courtiers tend to do when thrones topple and dynasties reel.

"How's that again, Glumphwortle?" demanded Vroop, beginning to frown a bit. "*All* o' me kingdom, you say?"

"I'm afraid so," said the green magician. "But, then, it really isn't your kingdom after all, is it, Vroop, old boy? They don't call you 'Vroop the Usurper' for naught, do they? Didn't you sort of, ah, grab the crown when the old king died and nobody was looking?"

"Well, I, ah. . . ."

"Quite so," said the Wizard cheerfully. "And did not your esteemed predecessor, the late King Haram, leave behind a son and heir?"

"Well—kerhem!—that is, . . ."

"The truth, now, you old rogue! Out with it: there's a good fellow."

"He did," admitted Vroop rather shamefacedly. (The throng of courtiers gasped, paled, recoiled, made protesting gestures, and otherwise did things to suggest that *they*, at least, had known nothing of this and were, therefore, innocent.)

"And was not the young prince exiled and outlawed by yourself, in cahoots with the Prophet Glibb?" the Wizard continued pressing. Blushing, Vroop nodded. As for the Prophet—who had been standing well to the rear of the crowd, hoping not to catch the eye of the Wizard, whom he also hoped was not of a sufficiently vindictive nature as to be angry that he, Glibb, had condemned him to an untimely demise—he began edging away as unobtrusively as possible, with the absorbed, busy and preoccupied expression of one who has just remembered important business elsewhere.

The Wizard reached behind him, caught Gamar by the shoulder, spun him out in full view of the crowd, and, with a dramatic flourish, cried: *"Behold your lost prince, Amar!"*

The courtiers burst into a polite splatter of applause, with a few muted "Bravos" from the rear ranks. Someone, rather tentatively, tossed a cap into the air.

Vroop, a surly, mutinous expression on his face, glanced from side to side thoughtfully, to where various of his guards and soldiers were standing.

"I wouldn't try it, if I were you, Vroop," advised the Wizard in tones pitched so low that only Prince Amar and Vroop the Usurper could hear them. "He who hath just thrust sixty Goblins into an enchanted slumber, would not find it beyond his powers to send half a hundred Yabites to beddy-bye."

King Vroop bit his lip, sighed, and said, "You're a hard man, Glumphwortle."

"Not as hard as I *could* be," smiled the Wizard, enjoying himself immensely. "I have it in mind to strongly urge King Amar to clemency on your behalf—exile, I think—perhaps a small, remote, unimportant barony on the Northern Marches, with a good piece of bottom land, and a modest yearly stipend from the Privy Purse . . . doesn't sound *too* grim, does it, eh?"

"I suppose not," said Vroop, grumpily. Then, perking up a bit, he heaved a huge sigh: "Well, after all—had a good run for me money, and all this kinging-it gets bothersome in time, what? Dad-ratted paperwork and red tape, and precious little fun you git out of it, when all's said and done—as you'll soon find out, I expect, me boy—Your Majesty, that is, I mean!"

Prince Amar said little, his expression a trifle grim.

"Expect you'd better go pack," he said. "Captain, perhaps you'll be kind enough to escort His Former Majesty back to the Palace, just to make certain none of the Crown Jewels become inexplicably misplaced while he throws together a few personal effects?"

"Yes, and be sure to count the spoons," chuckled the Wizard.

"Aye, Yer Majesty!" Captain Jork said, saluting snappily. Forming some of his soldiers into an escort, he marched the now Baron Vroop from the square.

"Well," said the Wizard, dusting his fingers together vigorously, "That about wraps everything up rather nicely, I believe. I do despise leaving loose ends dangling about!"

"Not quite," said Amar firmly. "For one thing—how did you know who I was?"

"That did not take any particular cleverness on my part, I must confess," the Wizard grinned. "I noticed how you hesitated, ever so slightly, when you introduced yourself to us back in the Jungles of Glash: you paused, just a little, before giving your name as 'Gamar.' Now, I knew you were a Yabite, and from the city of Shang, by your own report, and from your accent. That you were of a noble family and good breeding was evident from your appearance, demeanor and obvious refinement. You, yourself, told us that you had been forced into exile by Vroop, which suggested that your family must have been an extremely important one. No family in all of Shang could have been more important than blood relations of the former dynasty, and, as I happened to know that the Late King Haram had a son of about your age, with a name suspiciously similar to the one you rather hesitatingly gave . . . well, it was not difficult to hazard a shrewd guess as to just who you actually were."

"Um," said Amar.

"And almost immediately, when you displayed such extreme agitation upon hearing that Shang was being attacked by the Goblins, I became convinced of your true identity. Anyone else thrown out of the city into flight, outlawry and exile, would have been grimly pleased to learn of the peril faced by his foes, persecutors and adversaries. The Crown Prince of All Yab, however, might be expected to put patriotism above petty spite. Q.E.D."

"Um," Amar said again. Then: "Another question which has been bothering me. The moment I showed my face in Shang. I rather expected to be recognized by everybody I met—but *nobody at all* knew me! Not the guard officer, Captain Jork, who knew me as a child, or the magistrate Kang—not even that cantankerous old profligate, the Prophet Glibb, who had been one of my tutors! As a matter of fact, even that fat villain, Vroop, didn't spot me in the crowd, until you pointed me out. Did you—as I am now beginning to suspect—have a hand in this?"

"Of course, my boy!" the Wizard chuckled. "Did you think I would let you put your head between the manticore's jaws like that? Tush! 'twas only a minor ensorcellment to disguise your appearance, until I was ready to unveil the Lost Prince in public. It slipped my mind at the moment—that scar on your shoulder where they put the brand of the exile on you—or I would have hidden that, too, and you wouldn't even have been arrested. Sorry about that."

Prince Amar was looking at the green magician—a clear-eyed, steady, thoughtful gaze—as if just seeing him for the first time.

"You planned the whole thing, didn't you?" he asked softly—and it really was not a question at all. "You knew exactly what was going on, from first to last: you knew that you would find me in the jungle, a prisoner of the Wodewoses—at just such-and-such a place, at just such-and-such a time; you had it all planned, how to become Grand Shaman of the Goblins, and trick them into Shang, and enchant them, and overthrow Vroop and set me in my rightful place. . . it was all part of your secret plan from first to last, wasn't it, with no room for error or chance or luck or accident. . ."

The Wizard, for once, said nothing.

A faint comprehension dawned behind the eyes of Amar. For a moment—just one moment—an expression of incredulous surprise lit up his bronzed features. He opened his mouth as if to say something, perhaps to ask another question, and one of titanic implications: but the Wizard shook his head and put one fat green finger against his lips. Amar subsided.

The crowd began to break up, politely hiding sleepy yawns behind discreet palms. Amar mounted and rode off toward the Palace with an honor guard. The courtiers and officials hastened after him.

Dawn showed, a faint smudge of gray light against the east. Gloom thinned; shadows clotted. Vague pink light invested the now-almost-empty square (not counting the heaped and snoring pile of Goblins) with a sourceless nimbus. Abandoned, Vroop's empty palanquin lay tilted on its side: the slaves who had borne it on their backs sat cross-legged, waiting for someone to command them to do something, and, in the meantime, catching forty winks. The simurgh sat on a hinged warehouse sign, his head tucked sleepily under one gorgeous wing.

The Wizard took one last look around, gave a satisfied sniff, and walked over to the palanquin. Nudging the snoozing slaves awake, he instructed them in mild tones to bear him to the Palace. With a snap of the fingers he woke the simurgh, who fluttered down to perch atop the roof of the palanquin.

Then, in a small, lost, forlorn voice, Ooo asked: "What about *me*?"

"Oh, yes my dear *chela*—pray excuse my thoughtlessness: I'd forgotten that you were still here. Here, climb aboard—always room for one more."

The Wild Girl, looking sad and wistful, settled into place beside him on the silken cushions.

The slaves went trotting off toward the center of Shang, with the palanquin swaying rhythmically between them.

"But what about me?" Ooo repeated in a small wisp of a voice. "What happens to *me*, now?"

"To you, my dear?" murmured the Wizard, smothering a yawn with one hand, while with the other he fished beneath his red robes, finding the fat little black jug that never seemed to be empty.

He took a healthy swig, wiped the mouth of the jug against his sleeve, and offered it to her. The Wild Girl took a timid swallow or two, coughed a bit, handed it back.

"Well, as for you, my dear," he said abstractedly, "I should imagine that, if you play your cards right, you will probably be the next Queen of Shang."

"Reeeeelly?" squealed Ooo, excitedly. "*Meee?*"

"Really," yawned the Wizard, "You."

Dawn broke over Shang; and it was about time. It had been quite a night.

THE AFTERWORD

In Which, After the Usual Coronations and Weddings and Banquets and Victory Speeches, and All That Sort of Thing, Our Friends Part—Each to His or Her Own Particular Destiny —and the Wizard Goes Home to Mount Wu

The Palace chef whipped up a late-night (or early morning) snack, and the Wizard, Prince Amar, the Wild Girl and the simurgh dined picnic-fashion in the throne room.

Captain Jork reported that Vroop had scrawled his "X" on the Document of Abdication, and had ridden off, under heavy escort, for the distant Barony of Gunk, from which he would doubtless never return.

"And did you count the spoons?" inquired Oolb Votz, with a chuckle.

"Sure did, Yer Wizardry," said the good captain, blushing. "An' they wuz missing, just like ya said."

He then added that the former Prophet, Glibb, had vanished, although a robed and hooded man on a fast yale had left the city a bit earlier, accompanied by twin "nieces."

"That was probably Glibb, with the spoons," grinned the Wizard. "Well, with those two troublemakers gone, the realm is probably secure enough for Amar. Good work, Jork: here, have a snort—" and he proffered the fat little black jug to the guardsman.

"Well, now, don't mind if I do—jus' to cut the dust, y'unnerstan'!" said that worthy, upending the jug.

Then they all trooped off to guest rooms which had hastily been put in order for them. Ooo did not share the Wizard's quarters, and sneaked out of her own room as soon as she could. Amar's suite was just down the hall, and you don't have to possess magical powers to guess that the happy couple probably began the honeymoon a bit earlier than is customary.

The next morning, after sleeping late, and sharing a lengthy and delicious breakfast, the group found there were several things to be done.

Amar and the Wizard went up on the walls with megaphones to harangue the army of disgruntled Goblins, who were still lurking about wondering what had happened to The Unspeakable and his corps of officers. Oolb soon put their minds at ease on the question of their monarch's present condition: still snoozing lustily, Gluth had spent what little had been left of the night locked in a dungeon cell, and so had the others.

Then began a protracted series of negotiations. It was too much to ask for Amar to expect the Goblins to surrender, as the Wizard had pointed out to him *sotto voce*: a stubborn and prideful crew, the nasty little beasts would rather fight to the last man—the last Goblin, that is—than confess to defeat, and surrender.

On the other hand, they really did want The Unspeakable back—and badly. For in his absence the Royal Wife, Glub-Glub, had taken charge as Queen-Regent during the minority of the Royal Heir, Dung. She had already taken her revenge for various real or fancied slights, and old grudges, by having thirty or forty hapless subjects boiled alive in oil.

None of the Goblins were all that terrifically fond of Gluth, but at least they were used to him and knew how to stay on his good side. And almost anything was better than being bossed around, and sometimes boiled, by Glub-Glub. Since Goblins grow up slowly, they had seventy-nine years of Queen Glub-Glub the Vindictive to look forward to, before that little monster, Dung, could become King. No—all things considered, they longed for the release and return of Gluth.

But they *would not* surrender.

Prince Amar displayed his fledgling abilities as a statesman by suggesting (after only a few hints from the Wizard) a compromise solution. We will give you back Gluth and the Generals, he announced, in return for all of your weapons.

To this proposal, after quite a lot of hooting and gobbling, the Goblins eventually agreed. Of course, it was just the same as surrendering—since an army without its weapons is no army at all, just a lot of people—but it did spare them the indignity of actually surrendering.

So all afternoon hordes of grumpy Goblins and Trolls and Pixies and Dwarves and such-like came trudging up to heap their weapons before the gates of Shang. There were pikes and billhooks, axes and warhammers, clubs and dirks and knives, swords and claymores and stilettoes, maces and quarterstaves and darts, spears and bows and arrows, and lots and lots of rocks.

The Trolls had to yield over their battering-rams and the Dwarves had to give up their picks and shovels, and all of the catapults and mangonels and other siege machines were also surrendered. It took an awful lot of time to stack up all this hardware—even longer than it has taken me just to list the stuff—and the last stages of it were not accomplished until after sundown. But, finally, the surrender of the weapons of war was completed.

Then the Goblins withdrew to their camp and the Yabites came out and gathered up the Goblinish weapons and carried or dragged or otherwise lugged them all back inside the walls of Shang, where the Goblins could not get at them.

Then and only then did the Wizard remove the sleep-spell from Gluth and the others and release them from the dungeon. They were led out through the gates and set free.

Then the Wizard and Amar and the courtiers sat down to wait and see what would happen. Amar had thought it likely that, without any weapons to fight the siege with, the Goblins would just give up and go back home. But it was always possible that Gluth would be so furious at being tricked and enchanted that he would stick around, and maybe send back to Goblinland for more weapons.

It was too dark by then to tell exactly what was going on in the Goblin encampment, but there seemed to be a terrible lot of hooting and honking and gobbling and snorting going on. The simurgh, growing curious, decided it was dark enough to risk a fly-by, and soared low over the Goblin camp, returning with news. Gluth, it seemed, had beaten his wife until she howled for mercy, and had sent little Dung to bed without his supper, and with a stinging bottom. Then he had boiled alive in oil thirty or forty of his subjects who had been first and foremost in hoping to curry favor and also escape the boiling pot.

By dawn it could be clearly seen that the Goblin army was breaking up. The Pixies and Dwarves had gotten disgusted and gone home, and most of the Trolls had gone trudging off into the hills, figuring the war was over. And between them, Glub-Glub and Gluth had executed so many important Goblins, that the camp was divided into angry factions.

Finally, by mid-morning, the Goblins themselves began to decamp, most of them in a huff and not speaking to the others. And so the Great Goblin War ended satisfactorily—for the Yabites, at least. And the watchers on the walls all went back to the Palace for a victory breakfast.

There followed, in the course of time, the coronation in which Amar was elevated to the throne of his fathers, and the Dynasty of the House of Hong continued after the brief interruption which the historians of Yab thereafter referred to as the Vroopian Usurpation.

According to the ancient Yabite traditions, a bull unicorn was hunted through the forests of Voor, slain, and its liver (suitably garnished with green herbs) served at the coronation luncheon. After a twenty-four-hour vigil and fast Amar was swathed in white samite and crowned with St. Smogg's Crown, a spiked circlet studded with burnished bezoars, toadstones and adamants.

Half an hour later he married Ooo, and crowned her with the coronet of the Consort Royal. (Before this, of course, to make everything legal, the Privy Purse had purchased the Wild Girl from the Wizard for the price of ten gold *pazools*. The Wizard lost a *chela*, but the Yabites gained a Queen, and everybody was pleased.)

There followed a sumptuous and very formal State Banquet, at which King Amar and Queen Ooo had as their principal guests none other than Oolb Votz and the simurgh. The menu consisted of seventy-four courses, not counting the appetizers, and among the various goodies served were such gourmet delicacies as minced brisket of rosmarin garnished with sea-dittany, parbroiled marrow of mantichore with garuda-bird liver salad, and roast rump of tree-dwelling elephant with ecstasy sauce.

Ninety-seven kinds of cocktails, wines, champagnes, brandies and after-dinner cordials were also served.

The Palace chef, as you might expect, outdid himself.

The following day, King Amar held his first Council. He removed from office all of the appointees made by Vroop the Usurper, and in their place installed such of the Dukes, Grand Dukes, Archdukes, Barons, Counts, Marquises, Earls and Baronets who had served his father, the Late King Hamar, or whom he knew to be loyal to the Hongite Dynasty.

He begged the Wizard to stay on in Shang as Prophet, Peer, Prognosticator and Prestedigitator-to-the-Court, or in any other capacity he desired, up to and including that of Prime Minister. But Oolb Votz gently, but firmly, declined.

"My work here is done, Your Majesty, and I think that I should be moving on," said the Wizard.

"Please stay for a while," urged Amar.

"Yes, please stay," said Queen Ooo, who was of the opinion that she was with child—and hoped that it would not have green skin (which, in fact, it didn't).

"Let's stick around, what do you say?" urged the simurgh.

But the Wizard declined.

"It's very kind of you, but there's really no reason for me to remain here in Shang any longer, and, in fact, I have some rather urgent business up north, to which I should be attending," he said gently. "But my blessings upon your nuptials, for what they're worth."

Amar had a fair notion of what his blessings were

worth, and thanked him kindly. The Wizard continued—

"I foresee a long and vigorous history for your dynasty, now that it has been purged of the likes of Vroop and Glibb and their factions. In your time, my boy, the south will be brought under the banners of Yab, and in your children's times, most of the realms around will join with your empire, or be conquered by it. I foretell, in fact, a new Golden Era for this part of Zao: and I rejoice (in advance) for your good fortune. Be fruitful and multiply: and I know you will!"

That same night he left the Palace by a little-used side entrance, and was seen no more in these parts for a very long time.

Down by the river he called to him his fat scarlet lizard, who was rather reluctant to leave the nice squishy mud, but who recognized his master's voice. There to him, as well, came the simurgh fluttering.

"Sneaking out under cover of darkness are you, Oolb Votz, you sly rascal? And what about me?" demanded the simurgh, sharply.

"Well, come along if you must," said the Wizard. Climbing atop the lizard, to whose back he had affixed again his saddlebags, stuffed with all sorts of goods, only a few of which I have described in this book. (The Wizard, when he traveled, went prepared for almost any eventuality.)

They set off into the northwest. The moons were rising, and the wind was fair.

"Are you really going to leave those young people all alone, to rule this realm without your counsel?" demanded the simurgh.

"I believe they can do a pretty fair job on their own," opined the Wizard, admiring the stars. "Amar is the descendent of the hundred kings of Yab. On the whole, and for the most part, they were fairly decent men, those kings, and not bad administrators. Yab will carry on all right, without further help from me. . . ."

"And Ooo?" inquired the simurgh. "What sort of a Queen is she going to make? Why, the dear creature can't even read or write—!"

"Literacy is a vastly overrated commodity, among royalty," said the Wizard. "And as for Ooo, you will probably not have observed her hidden virtues, my dear bird: she happens to be the end result of over one hundred generations of controlled breeding. Her genes and chromosomes contain genius, simurgh, true and rare and extraordinary genius. . . and she will sire generations of great and mighty kings and conquerors . . . men and women who will rule with justice and vision and mercy, over a great empire which will transform the southern parts of the world for a thousand years. Don't worry about Ooo: among other good reasons, my dear bird, I happen to be her father. *And* her grandfather."

"And *that's* your idea of good genes, I suppose?" remarked the simurgh, after a pause. The Wizard smiled.

They rode on, underneath the stars.

"And what about Vroop?" persisted the simurgh. "Deposed kings have a way of coming back and causing more trouble. For that matter, what about that slick-tongued old rascal, Glibb? A prophet can be even more trouble than a kicked-out king—?"

"Great empires are tempered by adversity," observed the Wizard, taking a lengthy swig or three from his black jug. "Great kings are toughened by times of trouble. And strong thrones become stronger, by weathering heavy storms."

"In other words, there are rough days ahead for the Kingdom of Yab?"

"Peace makes softies," said the Wizard. "There are indeed great trials ahead for Amar's infant empire: but it will grow stronger and ever stronger for every tempest that it weathers. And our young friends will enjoy lively times and lengthy reigns: they will live long, and love deeply, and raise many fat babies!"

There didn't seem to be anything else to say, after that, so the simurgh didn't say anything.

But, quite a while later, he asked:

"Just why are you interested in Yab, anyway?"

To his considerable surprise, the Wizard actually answered that question, rather than pretending not to hear it.

"The Yabite nation, my dear bird, has a genius for poetry," said the Wizard dreamily. "The arts tend to flourish in times when a strong and wealthy central government fosters the growth of a leisure class—an aristocracy which has the time and the money to enjoy poetry. The empire which Amar will found, and which his sons and daughters—and *their* sons and daughters—will rule, will be strong and mighty. And very, very rich. A golden age of poetry and drama and philosophy and the plastic arts will result."

They jogged along on the fat lizard's back. Then—

"I have a weakness for poetry," the Wizard said, softly, by starlight. "It is the music of the soul."

"Well," grumped the simurgh, after a while. "That's as good an excuse for making an empire as any other, I suppose."

They parted a few days later. The simurgh wanted to fly home to the Ming Mountains to visit his relatives, the phoenix, the roc, the anka and the great zhar-ptitza bird. Their farewells were simple and devoid of sentiment: both of them knew very well that they would meet again, in the unknown future, and would share yet other adventures in the days to come.

Thereafter, the Wizard continued on his way alone.

For a few months he lingered in the Land of Yuk, which lay to the northwest of Yab. Then, after a time, he wandered north and east again, and came to the city of Ruh in the Land of Wizards. Here dwelt an enormous number of wizards, sorcerers, magicians, witches, enchanters, thaumaturgists, witches, alchemists, seers, sages, warlocks, shamans, lamas, bonzes, priests, saints, and various and assorted other wonder-workers. For about a thousand years now, these magicians had been attempting to found a colony of magic makers similar to that which flourished about the base of Mount Wu.

He was well known in these parts, if only by reputation, was Oolb Votz. And he passed the better part of a month conferring, conversing, and otherwise hobnobbing with his brother wizards.

But shoptalk tends to stultify even the most gregarious of us, and it became time to move on.

By slow and comfortable stages, the Wizard traversed the Jungles of Ghu, the Swamps of Hu, the Plateau of Wung, the Desolation of Abb, the Forests of Fuzz, the

Hills of Gaa and thirty-two towns and cities, not counting the villages and hamlets along the way.

In some of these he gave public performances in order to raise *pazools*; in others, bored, he used the old trick of turning pebbles into the elusive *sponduliks*.

Along the way, of course, he met some of his companions on earlier adventures—or their sons, or grandsons, or great-grandsons.

He had amused himself with many other adventures, such as the restoration of the Hongite Dynasty and freeing Shang from the Goblins. My reader will have guessed by now that I have chosen but one of the ten thousand quests and adventures of Oolb Votz to make this book. Perhaps not the most exciting or dramatic, but (I think) certainly the most colorful and various.

During these travels north he had many brief encounters and surpassed many perils and hazards and enjoyed many adventures I have neither the space nor the time to incorporate into this story. Thus I cannot tell you of his stay among the Pishogues, nor how he eluded the Hostniks in the Dark Wood, nor what answer he gave to the Blind King of Wugg, who asked him to define the purpose of life in ten words or less. Neither can I describe his adventure with the Follets, nor how he avoided the jaws of Norka, nor what happened when he was carried off by the Sluagh, or of the riddle game he played (and won) with the three-headed Ogre of Yu, or how he escaped the Witch of Iron Forest, whose hut hopped about on chicken legs like the hut of Baba Yaga.

And I have not the space to tell you of his philosophical conversation with the Boyg he met in the impenetrable mists atop Whitestream Glacier, nor how he talked the Stryges of Mount Ssu out of popping him in their cook kettle, nor the clever strategem by which he avoided the Giant Grumblegore.

Of his adventures with the Wilis, the Cochion, the Follets, the Magots, the Lutins, and the Great White Piast of Lake Shun I can say nothing. Nor of his encounter with the Vii, or Tulapin, or the Maskanako. The Spriggans gave him trouble on the Marches of Zor, and he only escaped with great difficulty from the jaws of cartasuciriargunan. From the cyhyraeth-hounds, he escaped by riding on the angelic horse Haizum, and the Bucentaurs and the Himantopodes (or strap-footed men) gave him no particularly sweet welcome on the Grasslands of Hon, when he got there.

But he was a great survivor, was our friend the Wizard, and when he couldn't talk his way out of a tough spot—which was very seldom, indeed—there was always his magic to fall back on.

His last difficulty on the road north was to pass through the Escarpments of Yoom which are, as many of my readers will already be aware, the hunting grounds of a particularly troublesome pack of senmurvs, dog-headed eagles.

Finally—he came home to Mount Wu.

It was the greatest of all the mountains on the planet Zao, was Mount Wu: eighty-six thousand feet high it was, and the crest of the mountain was invisible to man. In fact, the unaided human eye could reach only as high as its middle girth, where it was wreathed with clouds.

Here and there about the flanks of the Magic Mountain were built the various collegia of the several brotherhoods and fraternities of the magical sciences. And there were also the many schools of divination which clung to the foothills: Dactyliomancy and Pyromancy and Onomancy, which last is divination by the letters in a name; these schools clung to the southern slope.

To the northern were affixed schools of Capnomancy, which is divination by means of drifting smoke, and Cledonism, or divination by impromptu utterances, and Ornithomancy, divination by means of the random flight of birds.

On the eastern slopes of the Mountains were the schools of Catoptromancy, or divination by mirrors, and Coscinomancy, or divination by means of balancing a sieve, and Necromancy, which of course was divination by the dead.

While on the western side of the mountain rose schools devoted to the study of Aeromancy, or divination by means of meteorological phenomena, and Gastromancy, or divination by means of the interpretation of rumbles and grumbling from the human midsection, and the six kinds of Eromanty.

It was a magnificent mountain, was Wu: almost a world in its own right, with tablelands and plateaux and glaciers and valleys, and range on range of hills and foothills and sub-mountains. Not for naught was it called by the poets "The Crown of the World." So vast was it that the sight of man could not entirely take it all in at a single look, but must track back and forth, and traverse, looking from side to side, as at an entire horizon of the world.

Cities were nestled within its crannies, temples and towns huddled against its flanks, tribes and nations nursed at its mighty breast. Truly, it was the Mother of Mountains, was Wu, Wu the Mighty, Wu, the Home of Magic.

Wu, the World-Mountain. . . .

He was weary of his travelings, and he wanted to go home. It would take weeks, and even months, to traverse those crevasses and bridge those ravines, and ascend those ever-higher ranges upon ranges of hills and foothills. And he was very tired. Too tired to do it the regular way.

So he reached forth and, touching his panting, fat, scarlet lizard on the brow, right between the eyes—about where the Ajnaic Chakra would be on the Astral Body of a human being—he pronounced a *certain Name*.

And the fat, puffing, scarlet lizard melted into whirling, spinning, churning motes of bright red and gold matter—

Which recombined a moment later, but not into a pudgy hydrus. Ah, no, dear reader—into a brilliant-winged and golden-crested king gryphon, with lion's flanks and arched breast, and the mighty wings and hooked beak and adamantine claws of an eagle. A gryphon, with wings of glittering gold, and beak of gold, and crest of blinding gold. . . .

"Up, my beauty," he cried, "and try thy splendid wings. . . ."

And the gryphon rose with Oolb Votz clinging to his

back, squinching his eyes shut against the tear-making wind.

—Rose, and circled, riding the wind: rose in ever-steepening circles which orbited the World-Mountain;

—Rose, above the temples, and the shrines, the schools and the towns, the tribes and the nations;

—Rose, above the very clouds. Pierced the empyrean, the very stratosphere: until they were breathing the pure ether itself, the two of them, the Wizard and his winged steed;

—Up—up—up, they flew, mile upon mile, league beyond league, until the world was very far below, and men, and the affairs of men, seemed small and inconsequential, dwindling to mites—to atomies—to invisibilities:

And before them, out of the pure ether, upon the utmost and veritable crest of the Mountain there appeared a City, which melted out of nothingness—a City of Palaces, cut from pure crystal, studded with gigantic jewels, brilliant as the dawn and fair beyond words—fair as the dreams and hopes of men.

Upon the sparkling parapet, the gryphon landed.

The Wizard heaved a sigh and dismounted. He unloaded the two great saddlebags, and, dragging them behind him, shuffled across the shining pave and into the mile-high portal of the most splendid palace of all this Metropolis of Palaces.

There, gathered to greet him, were tall and shining Forms. Some were winged and splendid, and some were crowned with Glory. Avatars were they, and Manifestations, and Aspects. Thirty feet tall they stood, and so brilliant was their raiment and the splendor of their faces, that men would have been struck blind.

He greeted them with a nod, a wave, a grin.

They bowed to him, prostrated themselves—aye, those blazing pinions brushed the blinding pave as those crowned imperial heads bent into the glinting dust before the fat green man in dirty red robes.

He went past them, into resounding halls so vastly arched and aerially roofed that glaciers would have been dwarfed in these immensities.

He went through chambers paradisical, thronged with

treasures of jeweled artifice that would have bedazzled emperors and popes.

He went through suites and alcoves, antechambers and apartments, shining and brilliant with such miracles of supernal art as would have driven mad with greed the sanest and least covetous of men.

And in back of all this multitudinous marvel, this wilderness of wonders, this castle of the inconceivable, he found a small door through which only he could pass.

It opened upon a snug apartment, with a closet, a good, soft chair, and a fat, comfortable bed. There he dragged the twin saddlebags into a corner and left them, with a little sigh of relief. His sandals he kicked off upon the gleaming pave, and in their place he donned a pair of carpet slippers.

Then he strolled through tall archways into a small, walled, sunny garden.

A little marble fountain splashed there, and roses grew against the walls, and willows drooped over pools where goldfish swam lazily: very old goldfish, and very beautiful, and very, very spoiled.

He clucked to make them come, and touched each of them with a forefinger, and gave each a bit of food, and called them each by name.

Under a flowering tree was a lawn chair of wicker, broad and comfortable, with cushions. He climbed into it and sat back with a sigh. From nowhere in particular there appeared, upon a small side table, a frosted goblet and a tray of snacks.

He sipped; he nibbled; he leaned back with a deep, hearty, and heartfelt sigh.

And, a bit later, he took a little nap there in the sun.

And no one dared disturb him, no, not all the tall and blazing Aspects and Avatars and Manifestations:

For they knew that The God was in His Heaven, and all was right with His world.